A Matter of Trust

Brigette Manie

www.brigettemanie.com

ISBN-10: 1500710970
ISBN-13: 978-1500710972

Cover Design: www.ebookcoversgalore.com

Edited by Hazel McGhie

Printed in the United States of America by Createspace.com

DEDICATION

To husbands and wives who understand that marriage sometimes gets worse before it gets better...and the better comes when we believe in God.

Adrianna threw up her hands. "Are you listening to yourself? You're talking about the woman as if she's still alive. You're not going to let me 'paint her' with my wrongdoing. I can't paint her with anything. She's dead, DEAD. And if you want this marriage to last, you'll recognize that she is D-E-A-D!"

"If *I* want this marriage to last," he asked, his tone low, deadly, and dangerous.

Adrianna swallowed and scrambled mentally to regroup. In her anger she'd said the wrong thing. But she was tired of Cindy's shadow and couldn't take it anymore.

"You'd better consider if you even have a marriage. You have single handedly destroyed my trust in you by what you did. I don't trust you, Adrianna and if I don't trust you, what sort of relationship will we have? Not much of one. And if we don't have a relationship, my question to you is this: Do we have a marriage?"

Dri clutched her throat and tried to hide the tremor shaking her frame. Was he thinking of divorce?

TITLES BY BRIGETTE MANIE

The Banning Island Series

Against His Will

Tropical Eyewitness

Five Brothers Books

From Passion to Pleasure

Once in This Lifetime

Someone Like You

Not His Choice

Local Gold

The Seneca Mountain Romances

A Fall for Grace

A Price Too High

All Things Work Together (novella)

A Matter of Trust

Mahogany and Daniel

A Man Apart

Forever With You

CHAPTER I

"Dri, it's one o'clock in the morning."

Adrianna ignored her husband's sleepy protest to her awakening him. "I know, sweetheart, but I can't sleep."

"So I have to suffer too?"

"You do." She grinned in the darkness. The weight of the sigh he heaved to that remark could resurrect an entire graveyard.

"Maybe you should take some sleeping pills," he grumbled.

"Can't. I'm taking birth control, remember? It might interfere with its effectiveness."

He didn't say anything. Dri hadn't really expected him to. Whenever baby related talk surfaced, Christopher became quiet, withdrawn, or evasive.

"Although I've been wondering if that's what's causing my insomnia," she went on. "I got a new birth control prescription last month and ever since then I can't sleep. Maybe I need to stop taking them for a while."

She sensed him stiffen, and the tension in his next question confirmed his disquiet. "And what will be the alternative?"

"You could use something," she suggested.

"You know I'm allergic to that."

"Or we could try not using anything…" She trailed off and held her breath.

"Adrianna." Her name came out like a warning. "We've been over this before, too many times for us to do it again."

She knew that, but she wasn't about to give up or give in. In a few months she would be forty years old. She wanted a baby before then; at least she wanted to be pregnant. Adoption wasn't an option for her. That's what he wanted; but why should she settle for that when she could have one of her own, if only her husband would give it to her? But he didn't want to. Christopher was afraid that she would end up like his first wife, Cindy, who'd had an accident and bled to death when she was seven months pregnant. He'd lost both her and the baby. He maintained he couldn't endure that again. Trust in God, she'd told him innumerable times. Just because something bad happened once didn't mean there would be a repeat of it. But he was adamant and didn't want to hear anything about her getting pregnant. They'd been married a little over two years now. Dri was more than ready to expand her family of two. She just needed her husband's cooperation to get it done. Even though he'd told her how he felt about her conceiving and having a baby the traditional way, Adrianna had thought that with time he would change his mind. He hadn't and she was tired of giving in to his insistence that she take these pills that were withholding the one thing in life that she craved—a baby before her fertility ran out.

She scooted over, closing the space between her and Christopher in the spacious King sized bed. She fitted her frame against his back, pressing her breasts into him and throwing her leg over his. She kissed him just below his earlobe, letting her tongue linger a little and teasing him in the way he liked. "I know," she responded to his statement. "But I want a baby that's truly ours." She nuzzled his ear and slid her hand across his chest. "I want a little person that we make together." She trailed her nails across his sensitive pectorals, feeling pleased when they bunched beneath her touch. "I want a baby that's born from the beauty of our union, and one that looks like you." She pressed her hand against his heart.

His rapid heartbeat against her palm and the strength of his hold on her hand told Adrianna that he was affected by her words. The question was, had they moved him to see things her way, to yield to her will, to give her what she wanted?

"Dri, baby, I hear you. I know how you feel and what you want. But I can't take the chance of losing you."

Apparently her plea hadn't been passionate enough. "Christopher, women get pregnant and have safe deliveries all the time—many of them without complications."

"You might be the exception."

Just like Cindy were the unsaid words, but they echoed on the air just as if he'd spoken them.

"Chris, you need to trust God, and let Him take away your fear. It's like you're a slave to a past negative experience. You're denying the power of God to give you a positive future."

"Yet He chose not to give me one with Cindy and the baby." His words were bitter and resentful.

Dri knew he'd come a long way in his Christian experience; yet once in a while, when she brought up pregnancy, he'd reference his dead wife and lost child with anger towards God. She brought up the baby argument often. In fairness to him, he didn't show bitterness much. Dri knew he had a long way to go before he fully trusted God and even then, she was coming to believe he wouldn't want her to have his baby. He just could not get over his fear.

She clasped his shoulder and massaged the tension out of it. "You know everything works for the good of God's children—the good and the bad things. We don't know why it happened, Christopher, but we just accept and believe that God will work all things out for our good." She leaned closer and kissed his temple. "Look at it like this. After all you went through, you got me. Not to blow my own horn, but I'm pretty hot stuff."

His jaw moved, and she felt his smile. Adrianna kissed the corner of his mouth, glad that the dark moment had passed. She kissed him again and kept at it as he relaxed and turned towards her. When he gathered her into his arms, Adrianna wound her arms around his neck and arched against him.

"I think you're flaming hot stuff," her husband whispered, his voice early morning husky and after midnight sexy.

"And I think you're way past sizzling," she murmured, locking lips with him, her tongue getting busy.

He didn't answer, at least not with words because he couldn't. But he had a deeply intimate conversation with her, using a vocabulary that involved touching, stroking, kissing, and some very lengthy loving.

***

Adrianna felt guilty as she watched Christopher back out of their driveway the next morning headed for work. Her eyes tracked the

Dodge truck with the name Vibrant View Landscaping emblazoned on the side until it disappeared around the corner. Last night she had only meant to wear him down with words. But pleas or reason hadn't worked thus far; so when he hadn't withdrawn from her advance, she took it as a sign that it was the appropriate hour to implement a plan she'd been hatching for the past month. The doctor had given her new birth control pills. That was true. But the insomnia was more from not taking rather than from taking them. In fact it wasn't so much the 'not taking' that was tormenting her into sleeplessness, it was more the deception that she had decided upon a month ago.

Her cell phone rang. It was her sister Karen. Dri answered, "Hi, Karen. What's up?"

"Hi, Dri. Are we still on for lunch at Selena's today? You'd said you might not make it if you didn't meet your design deadline."

Adrianna was a graphic and web designer who worked from home. A lot of local work came to her from the Heart Haven community, one of the four towns in the Seneca Mountain area and a place with a growing writer and musician population. She did book and CD covers for those artists.

"I made it. I finished the website and the three book covers I had to do."

"Thank God!" Karen exclaimed feelingly while Adrianna's brows rose at the fervor in her sister's voice. "I just need to get out of the house. This stay-at-home mom thing is great, but sometimes I need a change of scene. If I listen to *Wade in the Water Children* one more time, I'll wade straight into insanity."

Dri laughed, knowing that Jonah, Karen's two year old son, loved that song and wanted his mother to play it constantly. Besides Jonah, Karen had a daughter, Esther, who was four, and a baby on the way. Karen loved her kids and had given up her day job as a Customer Service Supervisor to raise them; but raising kids wasn't like a nine to five job. It was non-stop, twenty-four hours and especially with children as young as hers. Their weekly lunches had become a ritual, and Dri knew Karen looked forward to what she called her 'mom on strike' time. Douglas, Karen's husband, usually watched the children while she had lunch with Dri. "Even if I hadn't finished, I'd have kept the lunch date. Can't have my baby sister losing it," Adrianna teased.

"Mommy, what's Jonah eating?" Dri heard Esther's curious question in the background.

"Eating?" Karen spoke into the phone distractedly, as if her attention was split between their conversation and what her daughter just said. "Mercy! Dri, I'll call you back. I think Jonah ate garbage."

Adrianna moved the silent handset from her ear and looked at it with a smile. She could imagine how Karen's heart was beating like it wanted to fly out of her chest at the suspicion that her child ate refuse. Toddlers at some point ate something that they shouldn't, and moms always reacted the same way—meltdown! As nerve wracking as it must be to think your kid ate trash, Dri wanted to experience that. It sounded a little deranged as she thought about it, but she just wanted to be a mother and experience all that they go through. Why couldn't her husband see things her way? Oh, well that was a moot point now. She couldn't convince him; so she tricked him. Somehow she hadn't thought she would feel as wretched about it as she did, although not wretched enough to truly regret it. She was getting what she wanted out of it—a baby. Once their son or daughter was born and Christopher saw his or her sweet face, he would forget her duplicity. At least that's what Adrianna hoped for.

CHAPTER II

Dri crawled through the second lot of the municipal parking, searching in vain for space. Finding a parking spot in downtown Mountain Spring at noon was as likely as finding a million dollars anywhere. Still Adrianna prayed that somebody would choose this precise time to pull out of a spot so she could take it. She was already ten minutes late for her lunch date with her sister.

Three cars ahead, a mini pulled out. Hallelujah! Dri stepped on the gas, her lips singing praises. The oncoming SUV, without so much as a signal of warning swung suddenly left and stole her parking. Dri hit her brake hard, her seatbelt the only salvation from crashing through the windshield. She sat frozen for some seconds, stunned both at the rudeness of the driver and the near collision. And then temper kicked in at the person's deliberate and reckless act. Dri laid on her horn and felt a 'Madea Goes to Jail' moment coming on. Where were the forklifts when you needed them? Stewing, she thrust the gear stick to park and reached for her door's handle, prepared to give whoever it was a piece of her mind about the dirty, not to mention ill-mannered stunt he or she had just pulled.

"I'm so sorry," a middle aged woman apologized. She rounded the hood of Dri's car, a baby cradled in one arm and the other clutching the hand of a toddler. "My baby's running a high fever and I've got to rush to the doctor's office. I grabbed the first parking I could get."

Adrianna felt immediately ashamed of her anger. She waved the woman's apology away. "It's okay," she said. "I hope she feels better." She assumed the baby was a girl with the pink bow on the child's head. The woman shot her a grateful smile and hurried towards the medical building on the left of the parking lot. Still feeling guilty, Adrianna drove on looking for another space. What did the Bible say? A fool lets anger loose, but a wise person controls him or herself. She'd almost made a fool of herself. She sent up a quiet request for forgiveness at the same time that an SUV pulled out of a parking ahead. Dri gave thanks and parked swiftly.

Early June heat and humidity enveloped her as she stepped out of her vehicle. She pushed her Ray Bans higher up her nose and settled the wide brim of her Panamanian straw hat lower over her brow. Stepping onto the brick walkway that divided the parking spaces, she moved at a quick pace towards Broad Street where Selena's was located. Half way down the road, her lace came undone. She stopped at one of the many town benches that lined Haley Street and lifted her foot. At the last minute she switched motion and sat on the bench instead of putting her foot on it. The town benches, shiny and green, had been freshly painted just a week ago, all a part of the mayor's summer beautification project. Their color contrasted beautifully with the large wooden tubs on either side, overflowing with petunias in variegated shades.

Lace retied, Adrianna set off once more, really striding now, her long legs eating up the pavement as she dodged moving bodies on the sidewalk. She ducked beneath low hanging branches of maple and birch trees planted at equal intervals along the way. Bending her head, she reduced her six feet height more than once to pass beneath awnings of restaurants busy with the lunch crowd. When she finally reached Selena's, Karen had a half eaten sandwich before her and a half glass of what looked like pineapple juice.

"You mean you couldn't wait a few minutes?" she joked with her sister, sliding into the opposite seat at their table by a window.

"I could but he couldn't," she retorted, patting her four month stomach.

"It's a boy?"

Karen nodded.

"Congratulations." Adrianna smiled, pleased for her. "I know that's what you had hoped for." Karen was tired of combing hair, and her daughter, Esther, had a lot of it. She told Dri that she couldn't imagine styling two heads plus her own. While glad for her sister, Adrianna felt a pang in her heart, not jealousy, but more of a yearning for a baby of her own.

"Are you okay, Dri?"

Adrianna switched her gaze from the other girl's stomach. "Yes, why?"

"You looked a little sad for a moment."

"It was nothing. I was just thinking." She gave Karen a quick smile and picked up her menu.

"Dri," Karen said softly, pulling the menu down so that she could look her sister in the eye. "What is it?"

Adrianna bit her lip. She and Karen were close. They shared the challenges and contentment in their individual marriages with each other, giving and taking advice from one another. Should she tell her sister what she had done? She decided to go about it in a circuitous way.

She waited for the waitress to take their orders. When the woman left, Dri propped her chin on her fist and met Karen's eyes. "Remember how I said that I could live with Christopher not wanting to have kids?"

"I remember."

"Well I can't." Forget the circuitous route. She raised her hands for quiet when Karen opened her mouth. "Yes, I know you told me so," she sighed, "but I thought it wouldn't matter. I thought that adoption would be enough for me, but it isn't. I want my own baby, Karen. I want to experience morning sickness."

Skepticism billowed Karen's eyebrows upwards.

"Well maybe, not that, but I want to conceive, to feel my baby grow inside me, to feel a poke, a punch, and a kick. I want ultrasound pictures, and I want to experience the connection of mother and child that can only come from putting my baby to my breast."

"Oh, Dri," Karen murmured, her voice sounding a little watery. When Adrianna met her sister's eyes, she saw the glistening of unshed tears through the shimmer in hers. "I'm so sorry that it won't be possible with Christopher."

Adrianna bit her lip and glanced away. "At this point it's actually a possibility."

Karen's eyes widened. "You're pregnant?" she whispered incredulous.

"I might be."

"Might? You're not sure?" Karen looked confused.

"It's too soon." Last night was the first time she'd been with Christopher since she stopped taking the pills.

Karen's face cleared and a wide smile stretched her lips. "So you and Christopher just started trying," she said with a sly grin. "I'm glad he's on board with your having his baby now."

Not quite, Adrianna thought. "That might be a bit optimistic."

Karen's eyebrows dipped. She didn't follow Adrianna.

"He doesn't know," Dri revealed.

Her sister's expression was one of total bewilderment now.

Adrianna explained what she'd done in hushed tones.

Karen's disbelief turned to horror as her sister spoke. "Dri," she said, looking stricken, "please tell me that all this is in your head still and you haven't implemented it yet."

Adrianna glared at her. Was she deaf? "I just told you that I already did it."

"Oh, dear Lord," Karen whispered, placing a palm to her temple and closing her eyes.

She remained like that for so long that Adrianna began to wonder if she were praying. "Karen?"

Her sister opened her eyes to reveal a somber expression. "Adrianna, you have to tell him what you did."

"I will."

"No, you need to do it now."

Adrianna shook her head in disagreement. "Karen, I don't know for sure that I'm pregnant."

"It's highly likely that you are if you didn't use protection. You need to tell him. He's going to be angry if you don't."

"He'll be angry either way."

"Adrianna, this is dishonest. It's duplicitous and underhanded. It's going to cost you your husband's trust. Believe me, it's not a good place to be. It's going to give you heartaches and headaches and cause a lot of discord in your marriage. I know what I'm talking about."

Adrianna couldn't argue with that. Karen was speaking from first-hand experience. She had married her husband with ulterior motives and it nearly cost her happiness. The thing was, Adrianna's action last night had been a last resort. She had tried to be reasonable, she had pleaded and cajoled, even wept and wailed for them to have a baby, but nothing had moved Christopher. He maintained that there were plenty of kids in the world who needed a good home and not enough people wanting to adopt them. He'd told her his position before the marriage and she had accepted it. Why did she want to change now? Adrianna had never changed; she hadn't subscribed to his way of thinking from the get go. Of course she didn't tell him that then and she didn't tell him now. Her child bearing years were slipping away, and her plan to change her husband's mind about them conceiving hadn't worked. Her back up plan had become her only plan. With her fortieth birthday less than six months away, Dri had felt like she was out of both options and time. So she'd acted, knowing the fall out could be great, but hoping to avert it or at least to lessen the effects once the baby was born.

"I hear and understand all that you're saying, Karen, but I had to do this. I had no choice."

"Adrianna, not to beat a dead horse, but you knew Christopher didn't want you to have kids. You knew about his fear of a repeat of what happened to his first wife. Why did you think you could change his mind?"

"The power of love. I thought that he would give me what I wanted if he loved me enough. Sometimes I wonder if he does." She said the words easily but Dri had been wondering.

"It's because he loves you why he doesn't want to get you pregnant. He's afraid to lose you, Adrianna."

Adrianna shot an irritated look at Karen. "Whose side are you on? I want a family, one with kids, Karen. You of all people should understand that. You have two and a half kids."

"And I'm very glad I have them, but if I didn't, I'd have been content with Douglas."

Douglas was her husband and pastor of the only Second Advent Believers (SAB) church in the town of Mountain Spring, one of the four communities comprising the Seneca Mountain area which was fifty miles west of Albany.

"I never told you I'm unhappy with my husband."

"I never said you were." Karen studied her sister's face, a tiny frown dipping her brows. Why would Dri make that statement and why was she looking guilty? She clasped her hands and leaned forward, her elbows on the table. "Look, Dri, I just want the best for you.   I don't want to see you going through unnecessary marital problems.   Think about this: Are the peace, love, and happiness with your husband worth placing on the line for a pregnancy he doesn't want?   Your hope is that he'll come around once he sees the baby. Suppose he doesn't? What then?   You'll be living with his dislike and distrust for the rest of your marriage.   Is all that unhappiness worth it?"

Adrianna didn't answer her sister because she didn't have a reply. Those questions had come to her in the month she'd contemplated getting pregnant without Christopher's consent. Like now she hadn't been able to answer them. She was glad when the waitress returned with their meal, breaking the uncomfortable silence that was stretching between them since Karen's last question.

CHAPTER III

Reno, Nevada

"Mommy, where's my daddy?"

Vivene Landry felt tears burn her eyes at the question from her five year old daughter, Emily. Until six months ago, she would have continued the lie with the answer, "I don't know." But that was before she 'died to sin' in the watery grave of baptism. She had to tell Emily the truth. She had been wrestling with coming clean, and the weight of her secret pressed more and more on her every day. Speak the truth and it will set you free. She thought she'd read that somewhere during her Bible studies. Vivene was a six-month old Christian. So she had a lot to learn and to memorize. Emily's father hadn't known of her intent to deliberately get pregnant on that night years ago. He'd been lonely and thought she was too. Loneliness hadn't been her main motivation, but it was her desire for a child that sealed her decision that night. At forty-one and with no husband and no prospect on the horizon, she'd made the decision to have a child and raise it by herself. Going to a sperm bank held no appeal. The man she settled on had been perfect. He was brother to her neighbor and good friend. The way his sister had raved about him made Vivene know he was the ideal candidate for what she wanted. She looked at the curious face of her little girl. She was adorable with her airplane styled hair parted down the middle and secured above either ear with a barrette. It was her favorite way to wear her thick, wavy black, hair. Vivene kissed her on the nose and prepared to come clean.

***

Montego Bay, Jamaica

Trey Livingstone walked slowly down the spiral staircase, connecting the first and second levels of his home. The marble tiles felt cool against his bare feet; the smooth stone balustrade felt the same against his palm. A soothing evening breeze blew in through the open French doors and windows, bringing the tangy scent of the ocean indoors. Save for the wind, no other sound stirred in the thirteen bedroom house that was now solely his. Two weeks after the funeral and the reading of the will, every family member, real and imagined, had left: Some happy; others not so much. The nature of the inheritance his wife had left them greatly impacted the state of their emotions.

Trey was glad it was over. His wife was resting now. Her illness had seemed endless with the intensity and persistence of the agony she had endured. Sleep until the Savior comes was something she craved during the final year of her battle with lung cancer. Pain, excruciating and unrelenting, was all she had known for two years— especially the final year. Just before she took her final breath, she'd whispered, "I'm ready." Trey had cried, his tears a complex mixture of contentment that her salvation was secure and sadness that the woman who had given him all that he had was gone.

Theirs hadn't been a love match. But over twenty-five years, he'd grown fond of his wife, and she had grown to love him, although she never said the words. They met when he was twenty years old and working as a janitor at a private university in Montego Bay. She was the head of the school's Business Department. At forty-five and unmarried, she worked long hours, which was how their paths had crossed. She was always in her office when he came in at nights to clean. Polite greetings lengthened into conversational exchanges. Pretty soon, Dahlia Powers, a woman with a commanding type of personality who wasn't abashed to ask questions, found out more about him than he did her. She learned that he was the oldest child with six siblings to support. With his mother sick with asthma, he was the sole breadwinner in his house. College had been cast aside until he saw his brothers and sisters through high school, although he wanted very much to attend. When she found out he wanted to combine his love for the culinary arts with his aptitude for numbers, she suggested that a business degree would be ideal. And then she made him an offer he could not refuse. She would bank-roll his education and that of his siblings. What was in it for her? Marriage in name only unless he wanted to change that. She was cognizant of the age difference and was realistic enough to know that women his age might catch his eyes, but she wanted his word that he would be faithful as long as they were married. Trey hadn't been attracted to her like that. Dahlia wasn't beautiful, but her body appealed. To a young ambitious man with a lot of responsibilities, he considered her offer a golden opportunity. He took it and changed the 'in-name' only marriage to a real one. After a year he figured she was the only action he could have so why worry over a little thing like attraction. In the twenty-five years of marriage, he'd broken his promise of faithfulness only once. His wife never knew of it.

Outside the house, he bypassed the mangrove and sea grapes on his way to the beach. The powder like grains of the Jamaican west coast sand filtered between his toes, pleasingly abrasive. Moving towards the water's edge, each footfall sinking into the softness of the sand, he lifted his head and arms, letting the breeze buffet his body. He'd gotten his MBA and realized his dream of owning his own restaurant—thanks to Dahlia. Now Irie Nyam was a franchise across Jamaica with one franchise to date in Miami, Florida and one in Brooklyn, New York.

With Dahlia's assets and his own, he could retire if he wanted to, but he was the type of person who needed an occupation. So he still operated a restaurant in Montego Bay, managed his investments, and oversaw his wife's real estate holdings. Royalties were still rolling in from her three bestsellers, which he had also inherited.

As the sea water swirled around his feet, he made a decision. Dahlia hadn't wanted him to remain single. He was grateful for that. He hadn't intended to, but receiving her blessing in that regard made him feel better about his private desire to remarry, especially since he had a specific woman in mind. He'd give it another month or two before he reached out to her.

***

Three Weeks Later
Adrianna floated out of her GYN's office in a daze.

PREGNANT! She was pregnant. The missed period, the queasiness in her stomach every morning over the last few days, and the breast tenderness were all because she was going to have a baby! Euphoria expanded in her chest like an inflating balloon. She felt as if she were going to pop unless she shared her news with someone. Fumbling in her purse for her phone, she nearly dropped the device as her hands shook with happiness. She dialed her sister. As the phone rang, her joy dipped a little because she couldn't share the news with her husband...yet.

***

At seven o'clock that evening, Christopher Reid laid the last slab of stone on the fountain he'd created in the middle of the property he'd been landscaping for the past two weeks. Mopping sweat from his brow, he pushed to his feet and reached for the remote to operate the fountain.

It worked! Cheers went up from those of his workers who had labored overtime to finish this project. Christopher's pleased grin widened.

"You did it again, Chris," Manuel Nunez, his project manager, praised him, slapping him on the back.

"God did it," Christopher said quietly, ever mindful that his creativity came from above. Most times when he started a project, he had only a loose idea of what to do, but as he worked God brought the ideas for results that kept his clients coming back and referring him to others.

"Yeah," Manuel agreed. "God did it." A Christian as well, he related to what Christopher said.

Turning to the others on his work crew, four guys and one girl, he said, "Thanks everybody for a great job and for staying over to finish this. We'll meet up in Mohawk Valley at seven o'clock tomorrow morning for the Pattel project. It's going to be hot with high humidity so let's start early and get out of the sun. If you're all agreeable, we can take an extended lunch at the height of the heat and put those hours back in during the evening."

There were murmurs of agreement all around before everybody said 'goodnight' and went to their respective vehicles.

After the others left, Christopher walked the perimeter of the Norfolk's backyard and gently fingered the petals of flowers. He bent to filter mulch through his fingers and brushed dirt off the brick walk, leading from the back door of the house to the barbeque and outdoor dining area. Canopied by a wrought iron pergola, the grill stood to the right on the exterior tiled floor he'd built. Patio furniture surrounded a table on the left for dining. He moved across the lawn, circling the fountain to the hot tub. Now redesigned, he'd elevated it two steps above ground and housed it in a cabana-like wooden structure. Mrs. Norfolk had been effusive in her appreciation and said it was the new favorite place in her back yard. He'd gotten two referrals from her for that alone.

Christopher loved working with his hands and had enjoyed Wood working classes in junior high. Two summers gardening with his grandmother had planted a love for plants and flowers in his heart. He'd gotten an accounting degree in college, but after enduring the nine to five in enclosed office space for five years, he'd quit and started building a business in landscaping. At forty two, he'd been in this line of work for about fifteen years. Even when he retired, he'd still do it. He enjoyed his work that much.

Knocking on the back door, he spoke to Mrs. Norfolk when she stepped outside, thanked her for her business, and got his final payment. Walking to his truck, he climbed in, whispered a prayer, and headed home to Adrianna.

***

Adrianna didn't like to cook and only did it because she had to. She had no reservations admitting that her husband was a better cook than she and had an interest in the kitchen that she would never possess. But tonight, Adrianna outdid herself, at least in the set up. She'd opted for candlelight and soft seventies love songs. The sultry sound of *Always and Forever* by Heatwave created the romantic mood with which she wanted to greet Chris tonight. Selena did the cooking. Dri only picked up the food. She comforted herself with the fact that she had to spend time on her appearance and on ambience which she felt she had nailed. After all she was celebrating something monumental. It was a pity Christopher would have to remain in the dark a while.

The key clicked in the lock, and Adrianna positioned herself so the glow of the candlelight would illuminate the wine red of her body hugging dress. Christopher paused at the door and whistled when he saw her. She smiled, stepping away from the table and meeting him half way.

His dark eyes swept her frame in a quick and appreciative once over. "You look gorgeous," he said, his gaze languorously sliding down her body again. His attention hitched at her bosom, which challenged the neckline of the dress to contain it. Adrianna bit her lip to withhold a giggle at his swift intake of air. He raised his gaze and the carnality of his look chased her mirth away. She gulped in oxygen now. "Please tell me you're on tonight's menu," he said huskily.

Adrianna passed her tongue across already shimmering lips, making her husband's respiration work harder.

"Absolutely," was all she managed to get out before he claimed her mouth in kiss so intimate that Adrianna wanted to skip dinner and desert and move right into their bedroom.

"Let me take a five minute shower, and then I'll be back," he promised, kissing her once more before heading upstairs to their bedroom.

***

Adrianna lay in the circle of Christopher's arm, purring low with contentment as he feathered light kisses down her temple and ran his fingers over her hip.

"Thanks for tonight," he told her, pulling her body closer to his. "I enjoyed everything—the meal, the atmosphere, and especially you."

Adrianna blushed and burrowed her face into his neck. The loving had been amazing.

"I'm still sensing that we're celebrating something, even though you won't say what it is."

She bit her lip, feeling guilty about what she was withholding. Should she tell him? Maybe she should. With him being replete with food and love, maybe there wouldn't be a fall out or at least not too much of one.

Running her hand down his smooth chest, Dri took the plunge. "We are celebrating something," she admitted.

"And what's that?" He sounded like he was smiling.

Adrianna burrowed her face deeper into his neck and confessed, "A baby."

The fingers drawing tantalizing patterns on her hip stilled.

"What did you say?" The question was hushed and incredulous.

Adrianna's heart gathered speed. She lifted her head a little. "A baby," she whispered.

Christopher sat up abruptly and turned on the lamp, flooding the room with brightness. "You're pregnant?" He asked, the depth of his frown turning his usually friendly chocolate colored face forbidding and ominous. "How?"

How did he think? She wasn't going to blurt out the truth unless she had no choice. She moistened her lips. "I think it's as a result of our making love," she offered, raising a tentative brow to see if that would fly.

It didn't help. With the glitter of what looked like anger in his eyes, the situation seemed to be slipping towards disaster.

"I thought you were taking the pill." His words emerged like they'd fought terrorists to get past his lips.

"I was." Technically that was the truth. She had been—a month ago.

"So how did this happen?"

"I don't know, Chris. No birth control is a hundred percent effective."

"You've been on the pill for two years, and it's never happened before."

"But this is a new prescription. Maybe my body wasn't used to it. Maybe it takes a while to be effective. I don't know."

"Did you forget to take it? You said it was causing insomnia. Did you stop taking it because of that?"

"No, I didn't." Another honest answer. She had stopped taking it because she wanted to get pregnant and not because of the made-up insomnia.

He threw off the sheet and got out of bed. Snatching his lounge pants from the floor, he stepped into them. Turning his back to her, he ran his hands over his head and then settled them on his hips. "We can't do this, Dri."

His dry, flat, non-negotiable tone struck a chill to her heart. She swallowed. "Christopher, what are you saying?"

He didn't answer and didn't turn around. Adrianna found her night shirt beneath her pillow and dropped it over her head. Crawling across the bed, she stood behind him and rested her hands on his shoulders. "Christopher, accidents happen. We—"

"That's precisely it, Dri," he interrupted, turning around. "Accidents happen. People die. Women die and babies too. I experienced it first hand, remember? I'm not doing it again."

Adrianna had been referring to unplanned pregnancy. What did he mean he wasn't doing it again? She searched his tormented gaze, trying to get a clue. Was he going to leave or divorce her? Or did he mean something worse? Her heart and mind filling up with fear and dread, Adrianna asked hesitantly, "What exactly are you saying Chris?"

He didn't answer and didn't look at her. He was looking beyond her, his jaw clenched, his eyes filled with painful past memories.

She swallowed. "This baby is here, Christopher, and there is nothing we can do but prepare for its birth."

"Maybe I can't do anything, but you can."

She recoiled. "I'm not killing my child!"

He looked at her now. Eyes previously emotion filled were now flat and detached. "I didn't think you would. Like I said, I can't do anything about now, but I'm not taking another chance in the future. Unless you do a tubal ligation, I won't be touching you again." With that bombshell, he spun around, walked out of the room, and into the guest room.

It took her about a minute to go after him. Adrianna was starting to get angry. Why did she have to do a tubal? She wasn't the one averse to a family. He was. Why didn't he offer to do a vasectomy? Foolish question. A vasectomy meant he couldn't give her babies. It would be counterproductive to her desire. Since he hadn't thought of it, she wasn't stupid enough to suggest it.

She laid a hand on the doorknob of the room next door and twisted. It didn't budge. He'd locked it! Locked her out! Adrianna rapped her knuckles on the door—two smart, sharp knocks. No response. Three more tries with the same result elevated her feeling of impotence. She couldn't reach him and didn't want to shout through the door because she had a feeling he wouldn't answer her. She wanted to look him in the eye when she spoke to him to see his reaction or non-reaction to what she had to say. She slapped her palm on the door in frustration, and slowly walked back to their bedroom.

CHAPTER IV

Chris laced his fingers atop his head and gazed at the ceiling in despair. This couldn't be happening. Not again. He could not endure the tearing, agonizing pain of losing another woman he loved. He knew how it felt to roll towards the warm body of his woman deep in the night only to meet cold sheets, to dream he was making love to her, and to reach for her only to find emptiness. The loneliness and sense of isolation were unbearable. Heartache and anguish lived with him night and day, occupying his every sleeping and waking moment until he screamed and howled so as not to tip over the edge into madness.

Christopher fell to his knees and covered his face. *Not again Jesus. Please, not again.* So many things could go wrong with a pregnancy, did go wrong, and had gone wrong. Cindy had missed her footing and fallen hard onto her seven months pregnant stomach. By the time they'd reached him, she was gone and the baby too. When he held her hand, the soft, flexible warmth of it was no longer there. The cold, still, stiffness of it was what he remembered until today. His memory colored his perspective with hopelessness and stifled any ray of optimism that there could be a positive outcome to Adrianna's pregnancy. *Please God. No more.*

When he moved his hands from his face, they were wet. Brushing the back of his hand across his eyes, he pushed off the floor and sat on the edge of the bed. The phone's blinking message light caught his eye and he pressed play.

"Mrs. Reid, this is Edward's Pharmacy calling. Your prenatal prescription is ready. Also, we just noticed that you didn't pick up your birth control refill for last month...although..." The woman cleared her throat, undoubtedly reaching the conclusion that Adrianna might not need them. Christopher hit the end button hard, and replayed the message to make sure he'd heard right. He came to the same answer that he'd gotten before. Adrianna had done this deliberately. She'd planned to get pregnant without telling him. Why else hadn't she collected her prescription? All along she'd been lying about taking the new prescription the doctor had given her. She didn't have insomnia induced by birth control pills. She couldn't because she hadn't picked them up from the pharmacy. Christopher covered his face and tried to regulate his heart beat, which was now racing out of control from anger rather than despondency.

He sat at the edge of the bed, closed his eyes, and pressed his clasped and fisted hands to his mouth. It wasn't a good idea to go into their room and talk to his wife tonight. His brain told him this. But every time he thought about the implication, no, the outright truth of the message, and about the reality that Adrianna had deceived him and knowingly gotten pregnant, his anger climbed to the point where he was shaking with fury. Rising from the bed, he strode to the door and snatched it open. He was at their bedroom door in three strides and their bedside in three more. She was curled up in the middle of the bed with her back to him. From her sniffles, he knew she was crying. Christopher didn't feel one iota of sympathy. His long shadow falling across the sheet alerted her to his presence. As soon as she turned to him, brushing tears away, he blasted, "You planned this, didn't you!"

Her confused expression exacerbated his temper. She knew why he didn't want a baby, had said she understood and wouldn't put him through that. Loving and trusting her, he'd proposed. Now she had methodically and deliberately gotten pregnant after her promise and her knowledge of what he'd suffered. She'd cast aside his feelings and selfishly disregarded his wishes to satisfy her want. She'd trivialized his trust and trampled on it just because she wanted a baby.

"You got pregnant deliberately." He made it a statement rather than a question, for he knew it was a fact.

The way she jerked and the fast flash of panic in her eyes gave her guilt away.

"Chris, please," she reached out to him, but he snatched his hand violently out of reach. He didn't want her touch, at least not anymore, not after what she'd done, and not after how she'd used him. "I can explain."

"Just what are you going to explain, Dri?" He demanded. "Are you going to explain why you didn't pick up last month's supply of birth control pills from Edwards?" Her hands flew to her mouth and her eyes widened in horror. Christopher clenched his fists to stop himself from wrapping his fingers around her neck. "Didn't know that I knew, did you? You should have checked the messages." His eyes scoured her face. His anger at her blurred the beauty of her soft peach skin and the sultriness of her long lashed oval eyes. "What are you going to explain, Dri? Are you going to tell me that you didn't have insomnia after all and that it was just a cover to make me think you were taking the pills when you weren't?"

She was shaking her head. Each movement was faster than the previous one as if she were desperate to deny what he was saying but couldn't find words to support the action because there weren't any. "Chris, please. It's not what you think. I didn't do this to hurt you."

"So why did you?" He raked her with a gaze so full of loathing that she recoiled with a stricken expression on her face.

"Chris, please try to see things from my perspective," Adrianna pleaded. "I'm almost forty years old. The older I get the less likely it is I'll get pregnant and have a healthy baby. I couldn't wait anymore, Christopher."

"So two years ago when you agreed to be my wife and said that it didn't matter that I didn't want children the traditional way, you were lying."

"At the time, I wasn't," she confessed in a small voice. "I thought I could live with not having kids, but now..." She trailed off, not finishing.

"But now you realize you can't," he ended for her.

Adrianna nodded.

"And you never thought it important to tell me about your change of heart?" he asked bitterly.

"It wouldn't have changed your mind."

She knew him too well. "So you chose to deceive me instead."

"Chris, I'm sorry for getting pregnant without telling you. I truly am, but life is not a self fulfilling prophecy. I'm n—"

"Sorry," he said scornfully, cutting her off. "Is that trivial word all you have to offer for the magnitude of what you did? You had sex with me, Dri, with the express intention of using my sperm for something I was dead set against. How could you make love with me, hold me, and tell me that you love me while you were deceiving me? What kind of person are you? You used me, Dri. You stole my choice, went against my will, and trampled my trust."

Adrianna felt like a flower wilting in heat. Christopher's condemnation highlighted the enormity of her deception, making shame grow within while she wished she could shrink into oblivion. She felt like crawling under the covers and hiding from the world and from him. With every word he spoke, she felt guilt like pin pricks, piercing all parts of her person and especially her heart. The truth was, she never intended to use her husband, but she had. The lovemaking that she'd so much enjoyed felt tainted now by his awful description of her deceitfulness. She needed to make him understand that while she withheld her intention to get pregnant, she hadn't approached making love with him with the clinical precision of committing the act just to make a baby. She loved their intimacy and enjoyed the experience every time. The level of loathing in his gaze told Dri that she needed to talk now to salvage this and she needed to talk fast.

She scrambled off the bed and tried to touch him again but let her hand fall at his scorching, *don't-you-dare-put-your-hand-on-me* look. Adrianna bit her lip and blinked back the tears that his action caused. Christopher had never regarded her like this before—with so much dislike and so much hostility. His looks had always been warm and loving. She didn't like this, couldn't endure it. Karen had been right. Losing her husband's love and trust and the peace in her home were not worth the pregnancy. She couldn't raise a child in this type of atmosphere. "Christopher, I love you."

"You love yourself, Adrianna, not me," he cut in bitterly. "If you had, you'd have had the decency and the honesty to tell me that you'd changed your mind about wanting a baby. You'd not have gone behind my back and gotten pregnant."

Adrianna felt irritability spark. Hadn't he realized her position had changed from the numerous times she brought up having a baby? Had he been that obtuse or had he taken it for granted that she would obey his wish forever? And with his unyielding position, didn't he love himself? Wasn't it because he loved himself and wanted to protect his emotions from devastation in case her pregnancy turned out like Cindy's that he refused to impregnate her? Wasn't he thinking about himself, caring for only his wants and not hers? Wasn't that loving himself? Since her objective was peace and not war, she didn't say what she was thinking.

"Christopher, I know you don't believe me right now but I'll tell you again, I love you." She looked him in the eye when she said it and repeated it for effect. "I love you." It had no impact on him because his look of disgust remained unchanged. Adrianna pressed on. "I may have withheld my intention to get pregnant from you, but that was only from fear that you would say no because you'd said no all the other times I brought up the subject. You asked me why I didn't tell you I'd changed my mind. I've been telling you all this past year whenever I raised the issue of having kids. You shut me down every time and refused to entertain it. I was at my wits end. I didn't know what else to do. I thought, probably foolishly, that you would come around once you saw a little person who was of your flesh and blood. I hoped your heart would melt when you saw me put our baby to my breast for the first time. I thought you'd have a change of heart when our baby's head popped out into the world for the first time. I prayed your heart would be so filled with awe at this miraculous procreative power God gave to us and that you'd be so humbled that He gave you a role in the procreative process that you'd find it in your heart to forgive and forget what I'd done to bring us to that point." Adrianna stopped and held her breath, hoping that she'd connected with him, praying that she'd touched him in some way, hoping that he could see beyond her crime, and earnestly praying that he would find it in his heart to forgive her action.

"You thought wrong." He turned to walk away, his expression more like granite than ever.

Adrianna had enough. Not in possession of a sponge personality, she'd taken enough of his pig-headedness and condemnation and she was saturated beyond breaking point. She let loose.

"Just one minute, Chris. Don't you dare walk away from me."

He kept moving.

"I'm not Cindy!" she screamed. Just like she knew he would, he froze. The woman was dead seven years and the mention of her name still had power over him. Adrianna was tired of competing with a ghost, tired of living in the shadow of Cindy's death, tired of her husband stifling their lives just because Cindy died. If he couldn't get over it then he shouldn't have asked her to marry him. *Maybe you shouldn't have accepted with all the skeletons in your closet.* Adrianna jerked at the last thought that came from out of nowhere. She squashed it and dealt with her husband. "I'm not going to trip, fall on my belly, and lose this baby. History isn't going to repeat itself. You call yourself a Christian and say that you believe in God. Then believe that He will protect me and take care of this pregnancy, Christopher. He has promised numerous times to do so. Take Him at His word and trust Him. And let us start living the abundant life He has given us, Chris. Let's start by taking this step to have this baby. Let's leave the past behind where it belongs and move forward with hope, love, and trust in God." She shouldn't have added the next statement, but Dri felt like it needed to be said. "And for goodness sake, let's not let a dead woman's shadow hover over our lives anymore."

Her husband whirled to face her. "Close your mouth and don't you dare talk about her like she's an object. She was my wife and I loved her."

"As far as I can see you still love her!" Adrianna shouted. "For two years you've slept with me in your arms but with her in your head, stopping you from giving me a baby."

"Don't you dare make this mess about Cindy. I'm the one who never wanted a child. No——"

"You never wanted a child because of what happened to her!" Adrianna interrupted irately.

"I'm not going to let you paint her with your wrongdoing. You knew my position and you went against my will and got pregnant. You lied and deceived me to get what you wanted. You did that and it's all on you. So don't bring Cindy into this."

Adrianna threw up her hands. "Oh my God, are you listening to yourself? You're talking about the woman as if she's still alive. You're not going to let me 'paint her' with my wrongdoing. I can't paint her with anything. She's dead, DEAD. And if you want this marriage to last, you'll recognize that she is D-E-A-D!"

"If *I* want this marriage to last," he asked, his tone low, deadly, and dangerous.

Adrianna swallowed and scrambled mentally to regroup. In her anger she'd said the wrong thing. But she was tired of Cindy's shadow and couldn't take it anymore.

"You'd better consider if you even have a marriage. You have single handedly destroyed my trust in you by what you did. I don't trust you, Adrianna and if I don't trust you, what sort of relationship will we have? Not much of one. And if we don't have a relationship, my question to you is this: Do we have a marriage?"

Dri clutched her throat and tried to hide the tremor shaking her frame. Was he thinking of divorce? "Wh-what are you saying?" she stammered.

"Right now, all I'm saying is that you knew how I felt about your conceiving. Yet you went ahead and did it. And the worst part is you used me, secured my ignorant participation in your scheme. Well, you know what? You can only fool me once. I'm not giving you the chance to do it again. From now on, I'll be sleeping in one of the spare bedrooms." With that he walked out and closed the door behind him.

Adrianna stood beside the bed feeling miserable, empty, and alone, despite the life growing inside her. Karen had been right. This pregnancy wasn't worth the loss of her happiness and her husband. But she had desperately wanted a baby and still did. Deep in her heart she acknowledged that her desire for an offspring was more than worry that her fertility was running out. It was also because she was trying to replace something she had lost a long time ago.

CHAPTER V

With the confusion the night before, Adrianna forgot to close the drapes. The morning sunshine poured through the sheer curtains, filling the room and turning mild warmth to uncomfortable humidity. Adrianna woke up feeling sticky and exhausted. She glanced at the face of her Movado: Ten o'clock. The droning sound of a lawnmower rose two stories from below. It was Tuesday, which meant Mr. Cross from across the street was mowing his grass as usual. Adrianna rolled out of bed and knelt to pray. She stayed still for a minute, having a lot to tell God this morning, and even more to ask Him to fix. She was at it for a good half hour. When she rose she wondered if God made sense of the haphazard things she'd said. Heading for the shower, she took comfort in the Bible's assurance that the Holy Spirit converts human groaning into a language that God can understand. Beneath the shower's spray, she went back over the prayer and her uncoordinated delivery. It was kind of hard to ask for forgiveness while in your mind you were justifying what you need pardon for. As hard as she'd tried, she hadn't been able to bring herself to seeing her act of getting pregnant as a misdeed. Wasn't God the one who told man to be fruitful and multiply? If anybody was being disobedient to that command it was Christopher. He was the one stopping them from having kids.

Like the soap's foam on her skin under the shower's spray, Adrianna's regrets about deliberately getting pregnant washed away in the clarity and brightness of a new day. Christopher wouldn't stay mad forever. She hoped as he watched her stomach grow, he would come to accept it. When he felt the baby kick, he would marvel at the miracle, and when his son or daughter was born, he would forget everything and the fact that he hadn't even wanted the pregnancy when he held this precious gift in his hands. Adrianna couldn't wait to experience all these things. It was something she had always wanted. Now it was going to be a reality. An optimist by nature, she stepped out of the shower and thought, Chris will get over it. We'll make it work.

***

The thought turned out to be premature. He was not over it an hour later when she called his cell. "Hey, babe," she greeted at his distracted 'hello.' "How are you?" No reply. "Chris?" Nothing. Adrianna looked at her phone's screen. Call ended. He'd hung up! She concentrated on breathing normally as agitation stepped up her heartbeats and temper stirred her up. How childish could he be? She dialed his cell again. It went to voicemail. She texted him but didn't expect a reply since he'd turned off his phone. She erased the sentence, *Stop being such a fool,* and wrote in more conciliatory terms: *Hi, sweetheart. I'm really sorry last night ended so badly. I want to talk with you. Every marriage has mountains of obstacles and this is one of ours. My hand is stretched out in apology and a quest for your forgiveness. Won't you please take it?* Sighing, she went to the kitchen and ate crackers, since the smell of the fried eggs that Christopher had made for breakfast still hung in the air, churning up her stomach.

Christopher didn't pick up his messages until he and his workers took a lunch break. When he did, he closed his eyes and compressed his lips to suppress his anger. Every marriage had mountains, she said. True, but she'd crafted this one all on her own. She had made this problem and now she thought she could work it out? They were going to have to live with the evidence of her choice for nine months, nine months of worry and agony for him when he'd be wondering every day if something would go wrong. And she expected him to forget this and forgive her?
He'd known Adrianna was strong-willed and the type of woman who always looked for a way around a negative answer when she wanted something. But she had convinced him that she didn't have to have a baby. She'd been open to adoption—at least so she had said. He would never have married her if he'd known she would end up doing

this. He had trusted her. Even when she started raising the issue of having kids during the past year, he hadn't believed that she would do something like this. He'd always told her 'no' and even though she tried to get him to see things her way, she'd always backed down when he ended the conversation. Maybe that's why she'd seemed to yield to his viewpoint so many times before. She'd had this up her sleeve. It had been her ace in the hole all along. Now she had gotten what she wanted and made a fool out of him doing it. She caught him this time; he wouldn't let it happen again. If it meant going their separate ways, so be it.

CHAPTER VI

Two months later

Adrianna braced her elbows on her work desk and held her throbbing head between her hands. Since yesterday she'd been feeling nauseated and wondered why the morning sickness she'd overcome had returned so suddenly. For the past two hours she'd been feeling feverish. Adrianna prayed she wasn't getting sick. She took her vitamins like clockwork and got as much rest as she could, but unhappiness had a way of robbing people of sleep. In the middle of the night when she should be sleeping, she'd be thinking about the silence in her home. It was worse than living by herself. At least then the quiet had been expected and she'd been used to it. But this silence was pronounced, unnatural, and painful, especially since her husband lived here.

As time passed since the night she revealed her pregnancy, his conversation had grown sparser and sparser to the point where he was no longer talking to her. She had tried many times to discuss the problem between them, but he always cut her off, either by a stinging comment having to do with her deceitfulness or by slamming out of the house. Dri stopped talking to him because she knew he would not answer. He never asked her how she was doing in those early days when she'd felt so exhausted she'd just curled up on the sofa for hours a day—unusual for her active personality. He never asked if she needed anything. Adrianna was convinced he didn't care. Had his love died because of what she had done? Had it been so fragile? Had he truly loved her in the first place? Or was his affection with his first wife? Adrianna knew it was stupid to feel jealous over a dead woman, but he'd talked of Cindy in glowing terms when they dated. He'd spoken with admiration about her even-tempered and agreeable personality. Adrianna had wondered aloud how he was then attracted to her bold and feisty personality. She wasn't the shrinking violet type. She was the type of woman who thought independently, went after what she wanted and got it, except for that one time. Every man likes a challenge, he'd laughed in response.

When she made up her mind to let Christopher date her, marriage hadn't been in her plans, but she had grown to love him. In courtship he'd been patient, thoughtful, and kind. He was the guy who brought her flowers, opened her door, helped her wash and curl her hair when she broke her wrist. So the man she now knew, the withdrawn, unkind, cold, harsh person, was a surprise and not a good one either.

Adrianna gasped and doubled over the desk as a tearing, raging pain sliced through her abdomen. Struggling to find breath, she cried out as another, more severe than the first, twisted through her belly like a blade. Cold sweat beaded on her brow and water started popping out of her pores like a spring bubbling from underground. She grabbed her belly and gritted her teeth to stop the scream the third time. It came out like whimper instead. Breathing hard she reached for the phone and came up empty. Where was it! She pushed off the chair to get her cell phone from the night stand and went down on all fours when the pain came again. Crawling towards the night stand, tears streaming down her face, she silently begged, *Please God, don't let me lose my baby. Please, Jesus, help me.*

Adrianna felt a warm, wet rush of something gel-like beneath her. When the warmth trickled down her thighs, she screamed, "Nooooooo. Jesus, pleeeeease nooooo." Sobbing hard, she grasped the phone and dialed 911 as gut-wrenching pains wracked her abdomen, while blood and life—her child's life—flooded from her body unto the carpet.

***

Eight o'clock that evening

"See you guys." Christopher waved to his work crew as he got

31

into his truck. He reached into the console for his phone to check his messages. He and Manuel rotated taking calls for his company, Vibrant View. Today was Manuel's turn. Christopher left his phone in the truck so that he could work undisturbed. There were seven calls, all business related except for the last one. As he listened to the message his heart began thundering and his hand shook as he fired up the engine and tore out of the parking lot of the Air Hills Resort property where he'd worked today. Dri had been hospitalized since eleven o'clock this morning. That's all Karen had said, but with the quaver in her voice and the catches in her breath like she was fighting tears, Christopher didn't know what to think. His mind whirling with all sorts of terrible scenarios about what had put his wife in the hospital, he tore down route fifteen, headed for Highway one that connected the four Seneca Mountain Communities: Mohawk Valley, Heart Haven, Indian Run, and Mountain Spring. Breaking the law times two, he redefined the speed limit from forty five to eighty five and dialed Karen while driving. She didn't answer. He tossed the phone onto the front passenger seat and forced his fear down. *God, please let my wife be all right*, he prayed, merging unto the highway and setting a new record of ninety miles per hour. He hoped his truck could outrun the cops.

***

He stole a parking spot from an elderly gentleman, shouted an apology, and ran for the Mountain Spring Community Hospital's main entrance. She had left emergency hours ago, they told him at reception. They had put her in a private room on the second floor. His heart beating faster now that discovery of what put Dri in the hospital was so close, he waited for the elevator, tapping a nervous beat against his thigh with his forefinger. The only hope he'd had was the fact that Adrianna was alive since they hadn't said otherwise at reception. At the door of her room, he had to stop and compose himself as memories of the last time he visited a hospital came back to haunt him. He walked to her bedside with careful steps. She was so still and pale. Although he tried to squelch it the question came, was Dri alive? With her eyes closed and her body so still in the bed, the memory of Cindy and her similar state stood out glaringly in his mind, only hers had been a state of death. But Dri was breathing. An IV was in her arm, feeding her medication. They wouldn't do that for the dead. Christopher dropped his head and gave God thanks, fighting the burning in his eyes and the aching in his throat.

"Mr. Reid?"

He raised his head and met the face of a smiling Caucasian man.

"I'm Dr. Metzger. I attended to your wife today and she's going to be fine."

"Thanks, doctor. I appreciate it," Christopher said relieved. "What happened?"

"Mrs. Reid has an infection called Listeriosis. Right now we're treating her with an antibiotic called ampicillin. That's what's in the IV." He gestured at the bag of liquid on the pole.

Christopher had never heard of that infection. "What causes Listeriosis?" he asked.

"Usually a person gets it from contaminated food and generally it clears in about seven days. However, people with weakened immune systems and pregnant women are at increased risk of being overcome by the infection. It presents itself with vomiting, diarrhea, and fever. Did your wife have any of those symptoms recently?"

Christopher shook his head but felt guilty. He wouldn't have known if Adrianna was sick what with the way they had been living like strangers in the house.

"Is she going to be okay?" he asked the doctor.

"With the treatment and rest she'll recover."

"And the baby?" The status of the pregnancy had been circling his mind since the doctor mentioned infection.

Dr. Metzger's eyes fell to the chart in his hands and he bit his lip. Christopher had his answer. "I'm sorry Mr. Reid, your wife miscarried. The infection travelled to her bloodstream and infected the fetus, causing a miscarriage."

Christopher could hardly breathe. When the room started swimming, it took a few seconds for him to realize tears were blurring his vision. He closed his eyes tightly. Why would a baby he didn't want matter so much? He had no idea, but the pain in his chest said that it did.

"I'm so sorry," Dr. Metzger continued softly. "There was nothing we could do. She lost the baby before the ambulance got here."

"Will she be okay?" he asked hoarsely.

"Well, we can cure the infection with drugs, but..."

"But what?" Christopher asked, tensing.

"But," the man went on, "she's going to need a lot of rest and care. I'm not a psychiatrist, but she shouldn't be left alone for a while. She's gone through something very traumatic and will need support to get over it. We did have to sedate her slightly so she would calm down and get some rest because she became pretty inconsolable when we broke the news of the miscarriage. She was crying and screaming beyond hysteria and we thought it best to give her something to calm her. Her sister, a Mrs. Karen Watson, was here at the time. So she'll sleep for a while." He looked at his watch. "Maybe until midnight in case you want to go home and come back. I'll be here overnight if you need to speak to me."

Right now, Christopher felt so numb he couldn't think of a thing to say. So he said, "Thanks, Doc, I appreciate it."

After the doctor left, he sank into a nearby chair and put his head in his hands while his shoulders shook with silent tears.

In the quiet of his wife's hospital room, Christopher watched the steady drip of the IV and followed the liquid's path down the line to his wife's pale, still arm on the bed. Two months ago, she'd reached out to him in a text, saying that her hand was stretched out in apology and in a quest for his forgiveness. He'd ignored that olive branch because he'd been angry and upset that she'd duped him into getting her pregnant. But while he hadn't wanted the pregnancy, he'd never wished for things to end like this. The fact that they'd had to drug her for her to calm down told him that the healing was going to be hard. He hadn't been there for her at all in the two months that she'd carried their child because he was angry and because, he now realized, he was selfish and thinking of only his desires. He'd wanted to preserve his peace of mind at the expense of her needs. Because he'd acted like a jerk, it was going to take a miracle for her to accept the support he was now prepared to give. Adrianna had wanted this baby a lot. She loved children and doted on her niece and nephew, Karen's kids, as well as the kids at church. Many of them called her Aunt Dri. Every Sabbath morning, she carried a bag of snacks for the kids to eat after Sabbath school. Several times after church the kids, the young ones and the teenagers came to her for food because they knew she always had something. Yet because of his infernal fear, he hadn't understood or hadn't tried to understand her need to be a mother to a child of her own. He'd robbed her of that. He didn't know if she would forgive him for it, but he was going to try his best to make her know that he loved her and that he was sorry that their baby had died. If he had to do it over again, he would do things differently.

In the depth of his heart, Christopher had a feeling that negative thoughts and emotions could help to effectuate negative results. Not once had he prayed with Dri for a safe delivery or for God's protection for her and their baby. No, he'd been too selfish, caught up in protecting his weak little heart and mind that couldn't let go what had happened to Cindy. Mentally, Christopher asked God to forgive his wrong and the neglect of his wife. He prayed that God would heal her from this tragedy and that she would find it in her heart to forgive him.

He studied her sleeping, composed face, beautiful at rest. Her hair fanned out behind her head in total disarray. The shiny black strands twisted and tangled, going every which way. Her black brows, thicker where they nearly met above the bridge of her nose, thinned out in an arc over each eye. Coal colored eyelashes rested above the shadows he'd been noticing beneath her eyes over the past few weeks. No doubt the strain on their relationship had put them there. The problem was getting to him too. Rest rarely came these days until the early hours of the morning. By that time exhaustion from the physicality of his job caught up with him and just about knocked him out. She moaned and murmured something unintelligible, bringing Christopher's gaze to her full, pink mouth. Something stirred in his chest and elsewhere, surprising him. He hadn't felt a thing since the night she'd told him she was pregnant, but then he'd been harboring so much ill will towards her that he hadn't been able to tolerate looking at her. With that load lifted, her beauty stirred his desire like before. Christopher was glad that his wife was alive.

CHAPTER VII

Adrianna opened her eyes with difficulty. She felt like her eyelids were attached to an anchor. With great effort, she lifted them. The room looked cloudy. There was a pole with a plastic bag beside her bed: An IV. She was in the hospital. There had been an accident. Adrianna closed her eyes and the reality resurfaced. She'd lost her baby. The tears started out slowly, building momentum, running faster and harder down her cheeks while the misery climbed in her chest until it rose to her throat and broke out first in a whimper, and then into full blown sobs. Firm, muscular arms pulled her against an equally firm chest. And the man she'd just wished for materialized. Thank God. "Trey," she whispered. "You came."

Christopher cradled his wife closer. "No, baby," he murmured against her temple. "It's Chris." The nurse had said she would be groggy from the sedative they'd given her and might say some gibberish when she first came around. He smoothed her hair and pressed his lips against her head, inhaling the passion fruit fragrance of her shampoo. He ran his fingers over the smoothness of her cheek and his thumb across the springy softness of her lips. Tempted, he kissed her lightly. She came awake, blinking into focus. "Chris?" She asked, sounding and looking confused.
"Hi, sweetheart it's me." He smiled at her.

Adrianna surfaced fully from the dream and looked at the smiling, chocolate colored man with the twinkling coffee eyes who looked like a mature version of Calvin on the sitcom, *The House of Payne*. Where had Chris come from? His face looked like it had been etched in stone when she last saw him. He'd bypassed her on the stairs in their home without a word and left the house bound for work. When was this? She looked at the IV bag on the pole, at the bed rails, and at the curtain partially surrounding her bed. Everything flooded back. Her lips trembled, her body shook, and tears started falling. She had been dreaming before. Yet the dream had been a past reality. She had miscarried then. Now history had repeated itself. What was wrong with her? Was she destined to be childless? Was it a curse? Or was God punishing her for her deceit this time and her out-of-wedlock pregnancy the last time? Tears streamed harder down her face as she faced the possibility of never having a child of her own.

This time when Christopher's arms pulled her close in comfort, Adrianna was no longer dreaming, but facing the reality that she'd lost a baby for the second time in her life. The man holding her and speaking words of love to her was the husband whom this morning had hated her. Now she needed him, wanted his comfort, and the soothing, reassuring strength of his embrace. "Chris," she whispered brokenly, "Hold me, just hold me." This time she got the name right.

***

"Think you're up to a walk?"

Adrianna shifted her gaze from the profusion of flowers Christopher had planted in their backyard to her husband. He stood there, watching her inquiringly, with their dirty dinner plates in his hands. He'd been taking care of her since she came home from the hospital two days ago. He'd stayed with her, attending to her every need. Today he returned to work, but Karen and the kids came over. Chris made that arrangement. He got home by six and fixed her dinner. Adrianna appreciated his effort, but she felt like it had come a little too late. Had he done this a week ago when she still had his child inside her, she would have felt like she'd been transported to glory. Had he done it then she would have showered him with hugs and kisses. His kindness would have made a difference and made her heart melt towards him. But now all his help seemed prompted by guilt. It came across like he was trying hard to make up for his previously awful treatment; at least that's how it looked to Adrianna.

Last night and the one before that, he'd stayed up late with her, watching movies that she loved and he hated. He preferred some good old fashioned shoot-em-ups to the emotional dramas she favored. Dri had fallen asleep in the middle of one of the movies and awakened later to find her husband asleep beside her with his hand splayed over her belly. She experienced a rage so profound that she almost struck him. He'd left their bed angry at her pregnancy. Now he was back after she lost the baby. He thought he could waltz back into the bed now that the cause of his fury had disappeared? Now he was touching her belly, same place that had housed a child he hadn't wanted. When she was pregnant and longed for him to spread his hand across her stomach to feel the evidence of their intimacy, he hadn't given her the time of day. Now he thought he could touch her as if nothing had happened? Adrianna had eased out of the bed and gone to one of the other two bedrooms in the house, making the silent statement that she didn't want him sleeping with her. He got the message because as she drifted off last night, she was vaguely aware of him turning off the television and easing off the bed. When she woke up this morning, there was no indentation in the pillow beside her nor evidence that he'd slept there.

"I guess not," Christopher said quietly and turned to take the dirty plates indoors.

Adrianna realized she hadn't answered him, what with her drifting thoughts. She wanted to go for a walk. The late summer breeze was cool and pleasant and would grow more so as the evening eased into night. It was a good time to walk, and she did need the exercise. She hadn't been able to go for her usual morning run since coming home from the hospital. The doctor suggested that she take a break for about two weeks and focus on getting her strength back. She had lost a lot of blood. "I'd like to go walking," she told her husband.

"Let me put these in the dishwasher, and then we can go," he said with a smile.

Adrianna watched him walk into the house, and the stirring of attraction that she always felt from viewing his muscles and the width of his shoulders didn't come. Her heart didn't flutter as usual when he'd smiled just now. Had she fallen out of love with her husband so quickly when for the past two months of her pregnancy she'd been craving his attention? The night she found his hand on her belly, she'd felt a rush of repulsion at his touch. That's why she'd left the room. She couldn't stand the idea of him being close to her and touching her anymore. Did she hate Christopher? Adrianna didn't think so, but there was emptiness in her heart when she saw him and thought about him. If she had to describe her emotions where her husband was concerned, she would say she felt indifferent towards him.

***

Adrianna stepped from her front lawn unto the sidewalk as Christopher held the gate open for her. She waved to Mr. Cross sitting on his front porch across the street, and stood aside as Glory Buchannan who lived two houses down rode her bike along the sidewalk.

"Hi, Mrs. Reid and Mr. Reid," the ten year old girl called as she pedaled past.

Adrianna waved and set off down the street slightly ahead of Christopher. Most people were at home at eight fifteen in the evening. With the weather so balmy, quite a few of their neighbors were on porches or puttering in their gardens. Glory's younger brother chased his twin sister across their front lawn, spraying her with water while the girl dodged and screamed with laughter. Watching them sent a bittersweet feeling through Dri at once again having missed a chance to see her own child do that. Not watching her footing, she stumbled as the sidewalk unexpectedly came to an end at the first cross street.

Christopher caught her and hauled her against his chest. "Are you okay?" he asked in concern.

Adrianna nodded and immediately tried to pull away. He held her fast. She looked at him. "I'm fine," she said abruptly. His lips tightened. She hadn't intended to sound so short and impatient. He opened his mouth to say something and changed his mind. He let her go.

They crossed the street and continued walking in silence. Adrianna didn't mind the quiet. She didn't want to talk to her husband. In the last two days, he'd tried to talk to her about the miscarriage; but she had cut him off every time, saying she didn't want to discuss it yet. Her intention was to never talk of it, at least not to him. He hadn't been interested when she was pregnant. Why did he care now that she'd lost the baby? They were passing

Williston Park, a tiny park in their neighborhood. The kids play area in the forefront of the park was empty. The playground closed at seven o'clock in the summer and the general park at nine. In the rear of the park, benches interspersed maple and pine trees, forming private seating for people looking for seclusion and quiet time.

Christopher caught her hand as they passed the entrance. "Let's stop here a while, Dri."

"Why?" she asked, tugging for release and not getting any.

He searched her gaze. Adrianna didn't know what he hoped to find and kept her expression blank. "I want to talk to you, Dri."

"Why didn't you do it at the house?"

"I tried but you kept cutting me off."

"And you think I'll talk out here? Is that why you brought me out?" The aggravation within colored her tone.

"No, that's not why," he said evenly. "Can we just sit under the trees a while? I have something I'd like to say to you."

Adrianna watched him mulishly for about a minute and then said, "If you let go my hand, we can."

The release was slow as if he didn't really want to let her go. She wiped her hand on the seat of her Jeans and looked in his face while she did it. With the hurt in his eyes she hoped he got the message that she didn't want his touch and that he shouldn't put his hand on her again.

She sat on the first bench they came to, at the edge, and rested her palm next to her so that he wouldn't sit close. He sat at the other end. It wasn't a very long bench, but he was far enough away for her. He rested his elbows on his knees and let his hands dangle between his spread legs.

Adrianna crossed her legs and let her flip flop hang from her toes, concentrating on the pink polish on her nails.

"I'm sorry," he started.

Broken record. She lost count of the number of times he'd said that since she left the hospital. What was he sorry for? For ignoring her? For not supporting her or his child? For treating her like she was nothing? For withholding himself and marital privileges from her because she went against his edict and got pregnant? Which one?

"I'm sorry that you lost the baby."

"*Don't* say that," she flashed, curling her hands into fists in anger. "You know you don't mean that."

"I wouldn't say it if I didn't, Dri. I'm truly sorry you miscarried. I—"

"You *never* wanted the baby. You made that plainer than the nose on my face. Now you expect me to believe you're sorry I lost it." She raked him with a scornful glance, muttered "Please," and looked away.

"Adrianna I understand that you're angry with me and you have every right to be. But when I heard that you were in the hospital I was scared—frightened nearly out of my mind. The message Karen left on my phone said you were in the Mountain Spring Hospital. I called her to find out what happened and didn't get her. All the way to Mountain Spring I kept thinking, you fool, you've been treating your wife like she doesn't exist and now she could be dead or dying. Your being pregnant wasn't a big deal anymore. With your life possibly hanging in the balance, my fear of you being in that condition seemed like such a trivial thing. All I could think, all I could ask God for was to make you live so I could repair or try to repair the hurt I've caused you these past two months." He stopped, shifted closer to her, and covered her fisted hand with his. She tried to pull away but he held her fast.

"I know you don't want me to touch you, Dri. And after the way I've treated you, I can't say I'm surprised. I don't deserve your understanding or your forgiveness, Dri, but I'm begging for them. When the doctor told me you'd miscarried, I felt like a bulldozer ran over me. My heart felt like someone was wringing the life out of it. I couldn't breathe, I couldn't think. I was hurt and shocked. I didn't expect to feel like that but I did. I knew then that I wanted this baby. I wanted our baby despite my anger at you."

Adrianna hadn't meant to cry. She had steeled herself against his words, never planning to let the poignancy of his statements get to her but they had. She would have given anything to have heard them before her loss. She felt more acutely the loss of her baby, knowing now that Christopher had wanted it too. Adrianna cried because she'd been holding herself in check since her meltdown at the hospital, trying to keep it together and fighting to put a good face to it, but the dam broke. The sadness and despair breached their barrier of containment, and her will power to keep her emotions in check crumbled. She sobbed—huge, wracking tears, letting out her pain and releasing her hopelessness and grief.

She let Christopher hold her, she let him hug her, and she allowed him to kiss her much like he'd done at the hospital. She permitted him because her loss, by his admission, was theirs together. And suddenly she felt like he'd now earned the right to share her sorrow.

CHAPTER VIII

Adrianna had been running for a half hour straight and she didn't stop even though she was a bit winded. On this late September morning, there was a chill in the air which was usual for the Seneca Mountain area. The cold came early in this part of New York State. The breeze cooled her hot skin. Dri raised her hand in greeting to a runner going in the opposite direction and to a cyclist across the street. Bayonne Park was a popular spot for sports enthusiasts in the Mountain Spring area. It had a track, a tennis court (indoor and outdoor) a pool, racquet ball and basket ball courts, and even a golf course. Along the fringes of the park, the town had constructed a two-mile road for walkers, runners, and joggers as well as cyclists. Adrianna had run around the park's track and was pounding pavement now on the road next to the park. She ran a wide circle around a woman walking a pit bull and veered onto the grass to avoid a mom jogging with a stroller. It was early in the morning and everybody had the same idea: Get out and enjoy the end of summer and do it early before the whole town woke up.

Adrianna kept going. She had some decisions to make. The major one had to do with her marriage. She had woken up in the hospital to find the man she'd married had returned. Christopher had kissed her when she opened her eyes and held her when she started crying. He had even climbed into the bed and cradled her in his arms—her six feet of slenderness ensconced in the arms of six feet of muscle. He'd spoken words of comfort, murmured endearments she hadn't heard in two months, and some she'd never heard before. He apologized for his neglect and told her he loved her—words she'd been dying to hear for two months, since she told him of her pregnancy. Bewildered and desperately in need of human contact and comfort, she accepted his attention and enjoyed it. Then three days later at the Williston Park, he'd brought her to tears when he apologized and told her how unexpectedly torn up he was about the loss of the baby. His confession that he'd wanted their child floored her.

Since then peace had returned to her home and they weren't acting like strangers anymore, although they still weren't living as husband and wife. He was still in one of the spare bedrooms. Now it was more from her choice than his. They had gotten close a few times, kissing and petting, but she had always called a halt to things. It wasn't like old times. Adrianna didn't feel the heat, the flashes of awareness, the tingling and throbbing she used to feel when Christopher kissed and touched her. Now she would classify it as pleasant but there wasn't any fire. A little worried, she'd spoken to Karen who diagnosed her with depression and suggested that she see a psychiatrist. Adrianna wasn't ready to sit in a clinical setting or on a couch and pour out her lack of sexual appetite to a stranger.

Privately, Adrianna suspected it was more than depression lowering her libido. While she accepted Christopher's apology and forgave him, at least she thought she did, memory of the way he'd treated her hurt. The disparaging words he'd spoken still stung. She wasn't sure if her husband truly loved her. How could his love have switched on and off so quickly? He told her that he loved her, but did he understand what that meant? He'd been angry with her because she hadn't obeyed him. You didn't love people only when they did what you wanted. You loved them in spite of it, just like God loves mankind even though they are sinners. He loves them so much, he died to redeem them. She needed to talk to him about how she felt but hadn't been able to bring herself to do it. She didn't want him to know the depth of her hurt, didn't want to be in a position of vulnerability, and didn't want him to feel like he could control her emotions. She'd let that happen with one man before; she wouldn't let it with Christopher.

Adrianna sighed and slowed to a jog as her street came in sight. She moved to a walk when she came to her block. The way she withheld herself from intimacy with Christopher was getting to him.

She noticed the frustration in his eyes and the strain in his face when she pulled away from his kiss yesterday. He asked, "What is it, Adrianna? Is it me?" She told him it wasn't and that she just needed time. That excuse would not last indefinitely. She needed to decide what to do about her marriage and her disinterest in intimacy with her husband. She had to fly to Jamaica next week to meet with a restaurateur who needed her web design services. Irie Nyam was an island wide restaurant, specializing in authentic Jamaican cuisine. The marketing director contacted her and wanted her to come down and visit the head offices for the restaurant as well as some of the individual establishments. This way she could get a sense of the ambience and sample their cuisine. They wanted both reflected in the design of the site. When she returned she would speak to Christopher.

CHAPTER IX

Montego Bay, Jamaica

Adrianna scanned several posters bearing names of arriving passengers and located her name on one of them. A short black man, whose white island shirt contrasted sharply against his burnt toast skin, had the card with her name. She went over to him.

"Hi, I'm Adrianna Reid," she said.

Large white teeth flashed, the color stark against his dark skin, making Adrianna blink.

"Right dis way, ma'am," he said, respectfully, taking her case and moving to the airport's exit.

Adrianna followed him into the parking lot and pushed her Ray Bans up her nose to shield her eyes from the sizzling Jamaican sun. As the heat sat on her head, she wished she'd brought a hat. She held her breath as the diesel fumes from several taxis tainted her air. She worried as she pictured her life taking a southward dip. Emissions control laws seemed non-existent in this country. She was following this man and didn't even know his name. She had forgotten to look for a name tag.

"What's your name?" she asked him.

"Sammy, ma'am."

Adrianna didn't like the ma'am bit. It made her sound aged.

"You can call me Adrianna," she told him.

"Yes, ma'am."

She grinned behind him and prepared to get used to being ancient. He was being respectful, she knew.

He stopped beside a shiny black limousine and held open the rear door.

"Thanks, Sammy." She smiled at him and slid into air conditioned coolness. She pulled her purse inside so that he could close the door and sat back, nearly purring as soft leather caressed her back and backside.

"Feels good, humm?"

Adrianna jumped, hitting her head on the ceiling of the car. Hand atop her head, she spun to the right, and her eyes nearly bugged out of her head. He was still tall, brown, and gorgeous after ten years. Time had been kind to him.

Her heart beating from fright and memories, she croaked, "Trey? What are you doing here?"

He smiled, slow, sexy, and crooked. Her stomach clenched and her heart stepped to a fast and wild Spanish Salsa beat. "Buddy was supposed to get you, but I told him I'd do it instead."

Buddy Marlow was the marketing director for Irie Nyam. "And you're what with the company?"

He grinned. "Last time I checked, I was the owner."

Her bottom lip nearly hit her chin again. Adrianna closed her mouth. Her mind raced. None of the informational documents—company history, founder and CEO information, or existing website—had listed a Trey Livingstone. There had been an Anthony Livingston and his picture hadn't been on the site when she looked or in the documents she'd requested from Buddy. She brought that up.

"Guilty. I told Buddy to change some stuff and had the IT guy take my picture down from the site. I used my middle name and adjusted my last. I knew you'd be looking."

"Why would you go through all of that? Why didn't you want me to find out?" She frowned at him in suspicion.

"Would you have come if you'd known it was me who owned Irie Nyam?"

She bit her lip and broke eye contact. She wouldn't have. She didn't answer—didn't have to. The wry twist of his lips said he knew too.

Adrianna started when a tinted partition rose behind the driver with a soft swish, separating them from Sammy. She shot a startled look at Trey. Had he done that?

He slid across the seat. Adrianna hugged the door. He erased the small space she'd made between them, pressing his thigh against hers.

She held up her hand to ward him off as he crowded her.

"How have you been, Adrianna?"

His husky voice tiptoed across her nerves and started a tremor in her body. *Oh, Jesus, help me. This cannot be happening. I'm over this guy.* "I'm married," she blurted.

He paused in the act of leaning closer, disappointment flashing across his face. "Do you love him and are you happy?"

She hesitated before saying, "Yes." Before the miscarriage her response would have been rapid and unequivocal.

His slight smile said he'd noticed her hesitation and read it for what it was: uncertainty.

He was moving closer again. He still wore Escada. The fragrance still stole around her, fogging up her brain like a drug, stealing her speech and her reason. "I just lost a baby," she whispered in a weak attempt to make him keep his distance while she watched his full, wide mouth and wondered why she felt so hungry.

"Oh, baby, I'm so sorry," he murmured, his voice more gravelly than before.

Adrianna jumped as his large hand settled over her belly and slid across the fabric of her cotton dress in a comforting caress.

"So sorry," he repeated and covered her mouth in a kiss that robbed her of what scant sense she had left.

***

Adrianna brushed her teeth about six times to remove Trey's taste from her mouth. She changed her clothes and put them in the hotel's laundry bag so the fragrance of his cologne wouldn't remind her that she'd succumbed to stupidity and to sin. Her brain didn't let her get away with the final one. She tried to reason that she hadn't slept with him. It had only been a kiss. But she hadn't pulled away, hadn't fought to get out of his embrace, and had enjoyed it while it lasted. The recriminations and guilt had come afterwards, but they should have come immediately. A man who looks after a woman with lust is guilty of committing adultery with her in his heart. The Biblical admonition in Matthew spoke like an audio Bible reading in her head. It was so clear. And the warning was unisex.

Oh, God, please forgive me! Adrianna covered her face and

sank down on the edge of the massive King-sized bed in the suite Trey reserved for her. *His company* reserved, she amended in her head. Ten years ago when she had fallen for him, she hadn't known he was married. He wasn't in the church. Back then she had one foot in the church doors and one foot out. So dating him hadn't been a problem for her. But she had drawn the line at being with a married man and walked away with a broken heart and his baby. She'd been prepared to have it solo, but she'd miscarried then too. Adrianna refused to think about that now. She crumpled on the bed and curled into herself. How had her life gotten so complicated in just three months? Things had moved from happiness to deceiving her husband, and then losing her baby to now possibly losing her marriage. Separation or divorce seemed probable, what with the way her desire for her husband had spiraled downwards while want for Trey had exploded and skyrocketed.

On the last stretch of the journey to the hotel, Adrianna hadn't been able to talk. Trey's kiss rendered her speechless. Her head and heart filled with guilt as she tried to grapple with the attraction that had flared as if time hadn't passed since she loved him. He'd filled the silence with the bombshell that his wife was dead for three months now. Dri had closed her eyes and wondered at the vagaries of life. When she'd wanted him and he her, he hadn't been free. Now they'd met again and she was the one tied down. That's how she'd been feeling before she left New York to come down here—chained and trapped to a man she no longer knew if she loved. This trip had given her the getaway that she needed to think. Now Trey's presence was muddying her brain and making it hard for her to do so.

While she shouldn't, Dri compared the two men. They appealed in different ways. Trey had charm, a mesmerizing smile, and an intensely intimate look that struck the word 'no' from a woman's vocabulary. When he entered a room, his face and his body were like physical magnets for the female eye. Beyond that, he'd treated her like every woman wanted to be treated—special. He called her, sent her flowers, sang for her, and when the doors closed at night... Adrianna slammed the doors in her head, knowing that going there would be past dangerous.

Now her husband couldn't hold a note and the one time he'd tried to sing her a love song, she'd kissed him to shut him up. But

Adrianna had felt special that he had tried since he knew she loved music and in particular she adored the one he sang, *I Just Called to Say I Love You* by Stevie Wonder. Physically, he was appealing, chocolate to Trey's honey brown. In a contest, though, Trey would beat him hands down in the looks department.

She hadn't even liked Christopher when he started flirting with her and had rebuffed him too many times to count. When Christopher Reid wanted something though, he didn't stop until he got it. He had worn her down and after he kissed her once, by cornering her, she came back for more and a friendship started between them that grew into a marriage. Adrianna blinked, realizing that's what was missing in her marriage now—the friendship, the ease they had with each other, the laughter, and the playfulness. She missed those. Since he'd quit on her with the pregnancy, all that had ceased. He'd been trying to bring it back, but Adrianna couldn't find it in herself to respond because it felt fraudulent, as if he were trying too hard. She missed the friendship, so why didn't she miss the intimacy?

Before the pregnancy she and Chris prayed together. He'd stopped doing that. Adrianna missed that too. Their love had been built with the desire, the friendship, and their commitment to Christ. Without all those parts, the relationship was unbalanced she realized.

After Trey, she'd gotten re-baptized and gotten serious with her faith. Christopher hadn't been of the faith when she first met him, which was one of the reasons she'd hesitated in dating him. But then her brother-in-law had baptized him and things had progressed from there.

Adrianna sighed and wished her problems would float away like an exhalation. She sat up and looked around, taking in the opulence of the suite for the first time. When she'd rushed in earlier, she'd hardly noticed anything. Her sole thought had been to cleanse her mouth and her body of her sin with Trey. The ampleness of the Laurel poster bed suggested that it was created with company in mind. She would be flying solo tonight. She wasn't that crazy. The bronze and gold pillows picked up the colors of the heavy drapes partially obscuring the French doors, leading out onto the eighth floor balcony. From out there the aqua and blue blend of the Caribbean Sea looked magnificent. A ruby bordered Isfahan rug, with its ivory center sporting an interwoven design of flowers, leaves, and vines, covered the majority of floor to the left of the bed. A coffee table, the same mahogany hue of the bed, sat in the center of the rug with an antique armchair on either side. The quality of the furnishings and the richness of the window treatments and accents in the room suggested that Trey's company must be doing well to have put her in accommodations as expensive as this. She was supposed to be here seven days. Adrianna had been looking forward to exploring Irie Nyam's restaurants—the cuisine, the customers, and the employees so that she could get a sense of the place and feed her creativity for the website design. That meant seven days in Trey's company. After an hour, she wasn't sure that spending more time with him than she already had was a good idea. Maybe she should quit and just go home. She would be losing a lot of money though. But was it worth the risk?

CHAPTER X

Her cell phone was ringing for real, Adrianna realized, blinking sleep away and catching the call on the final ring.

"Hello," she spoke hoarsely into the phone.

"Hi, Dri, sorry to wake you up."

Christopher! Adrianna squeezed her lids closed. She hadn't called her husband—hadn't taken time to do it, although she'd spent plenty of time kissing another man. "Hi, Chris. Sorry I forgot to call," she said guiltily.

"It's okay. I just wanted to make sure you got there safely."

She swallowed at the caring in his voice. Could her guilt get any worse? "I'm fine." *Not!* "How are you?"

The silence following that seemed to echo with the questions, *Are you really asking me that? Do you even care?* "Do you really want to know?" he asked.

Adrianna sighed inaudibly, knowing that her non-response to his good-bye kiss at the airport and her evasion of his advances led to this question. "I wouldn't have asked otherwise," she answered him.

"I miss you, Dri."

She caught her breath at the husky admission. Adrianna hadn't expected that. His honesty put an ache in her heart and augmented her guilt at what she'd done with Trey.

"I'm not trying to put pressure on you to feel something for me." He laughed but it was a bitter sound. "Truth is I'm not sure you feel anything anymore. But I want you to know that I love you, Adrianna, and the next seven days are going to be lonely without you."

Adrianna didn't know what to say. The natural response would have been to reciprocate his feelings. Right now, though, her emotions were all over the place, so much so that *she* was confused.

"The phone isn't the best place to have this conversation, but if I don't talk to you now, I don't think I'll last until you come back."

What was he talking about?

"I know I hurt you, Adrianna. I hurt you badly. I couldn't see past my fear and ignored your need to have a child of your own. That was selfish, and I regret realizing that too late. I know you're having trouble forgetting how I treated you. All I'm asking is that you give us a chance, Dri. I know you don't want me to touch you. I see your reaction when I do, and I know you despise me."

"No, Chris," she interrupted. "I don't despise you."

"You pull away from my touch as if you can't stand it. You barely respond to my kisses, and if I try to touch you in an intimate way, you push my hands away. What else would you call it other than disgust?"

She didn't say anything for a while. What could she say? He was right. She didn't want his touch. Dri moistened her lips and answered him, "Chris, it's complicated."

"How? Talk to me please, Dri. I really want to fix this."

"Since I lost the baby, I've-I've..." She trailed off, not knowing how to tell him her desire was gone. That wasn't quite true. She'd experienced a lot of crackle and spark around Trey.

"You've what?" he prompted.

"I've not been able to feel anything."

Silence reigned on the line for a little.

"Do you think that's because you lost the baby or because of me?" His voice came across the line sounding strained.

Adrianna didn't want to hurt him more, but he'd started this conversation and he was right. They needed to talk about the problem between them. "Chris, I want to say this carefully but forgive me if it comes out wrong. I know or I should say I have the sense that your remorse for how you treated me is genuine. Yet I'm finding it hard to accept that it took the loss of our baby for you to get to that point. Sometimes I think that if I was still pregnant, you'd still be treating me like trash." Adrianna propped her head on her fist and took a deep breath. "Do you know how many days and nights I wished you'd at least ask me how I felt? In the beginning it was really hard for me. I was exhausted all the time. Everything I smelled made me want to throw up. I know you noticed how I used to loll around, sit on the couch and watch TV. That's not me. Yet you never asked me how I was doing. Now, suddenly when the baby's gone, you have an about face and shower me with all the attention you didn't give before. I'm sorry, but it's a little hard for me to accept it now.

"I feel like you were punishing me with silence and neglect when I was pregnant. I feel as if you were meting out justice for my wrongdoing, for daring to disobey your edict not to get pregnant. You can't love a person selectively, Christopher. You have to love them in spite of what they do. The way I see it is that you loved me as long as I was your good, obedient wife who took her birth control pills and never got pregnant. But the moment I ceased to be that you no longer loved me. Now that I'm un-pregnant, I'm worthy of your love and attention. I'm sorry but it's just not cutting it for me." Adrianna stopped because her breath was catching, making speech difficult, and her heart was beating fast with the passion and depth of how she felt on this matter.

The silence on the phone had a deafening decibel. When Christopher finally said something, he sounded grave and very sober. "I'm glad you told me how you feel. I can see how my yo-yo behavior could give the impression that I only care about you if you bend to my will. That's not the case, Adrianna. I loved you then but stupidly let anger and fear dominate my mind, dimming the love I had for you. It's sort of hard to understand, I know. Your ending up in the hospital was a mighty wake up slap for me. I called myself every kind of idiot for how I treated you. When faced with the possibility of harm coming to you and losing you, I wished I'd taken time over the previous two months to tell you that I love you. I wished we were on speaking terms. I wished I hadn't isolated you. I made a serious mistake, Dri, one which I don't intend to repeat. It's going to be hard for you to swallow, hard for you to believe, but give me one chance to show you I can be a man worthy of your love."

Adrianna shook her head. "Christopher, my head is telling me to give you that chance, but I'm not feeling it in my heart."

"Are you saying then that we don't have a future?"

"I don't know Chris."

"So you don't love me anymore." His voice had gone flat and toneless.

"It's hard to say when I can't feel anything."

"Dri, I love you. Even when we had differences between us I never stopped loving you. Are you saying that in a few short months your love for me died?"

You killed it, she thought. She glanced at her watch: seven o'clock. She was meeting Trey for dinner, a business dinner he'd said, at eight o'clock. "Chris, you were right. We shouldn't have this conversation over the phone, especially not about our future. Whe——"

"What do I need to do to earn your love again?" he interrupted her, his voice tight.

Was he upset? She hoped not. As far as she was concerned he didn't have the right to be.

"Christopher, let's finish this when I get home."

"What do I need to do?" he repeated.

"I don't think there's anything you can do."

"It sounds like you're not willing to give us a chance," he said quietly.

"Chris," she sighed tiredly, "I think I just need time to sort out my head."

"How much time?"

Adrianna got irritated. Why was he pressing her? "I don't know. Three months, six months, forever, I don't know."

"Is it that you need time to sort out your head as you put it or do you want to make me pay?"

He sounded like his temper was on simmer. Adrianna got angry. He wasn't entitled to a thing, but he was talking as if he were. She owed him nothing. His neglect had brought this about. His isolation had suffocated her affection. He'd ignored her for two long months and left her bereft of his affection. She'd had to wait it out. Out of patience with him and out of good humor, she snapped, "Yes, you deserve to hang in the balance just like you did to me when you ignored me for two long months. Two months when I needed your touch, your love, your words of forgiveness, your comfort and your understanding. I had to wait and suffer until it pleased you to acknowledge me again. So why shouldn't you wait now that the shoe is on the other foot?"

"So the real reason for your coldness has come out," he responded to her outburst, his voice chilly. "You're trying to punish me because I hurt you. I apologized, Dri. I've done all I can to show you that I regret how I treated you and that I'm sorry for the loss of the baby. I sat up with you nights when you couldn't sleep after the miscarriage, even though I was exhausted and had work the next day. I've tried to do everything in that house domestically to make sure you have enough rest. I've told you more times than I can count that I love you. I've tried to come close but you won't let me. What more do you want from me, Dri? My blood? Is that it? What do you want me to do to prove to you that I'm sorry?" He didn't raise his voice, but his anger vibrated through the phone nevertheless. His words came out hard and forced like he spoke through his teeth.

Adrianna had enough of this conversation. "Nothing. There's nothing that I want you to do and nothing that I want from you, Christopher."

After some beats of silence, he said quietly, "It sounds like there's nothing left to discuss."

"So it seems."

"Okay, when you come back, we can talk about how we want to end this."

He rang off while her thoughts were still scrambling after that bombshell. He wanted to end the marriage? Adrianna's heart started galloping in fear. She hadn't thought that it would end like this. She didn't want to be alone. But what did she really expect after not giving him any sign of hope or encouragement? As the conversation rewound fast in her head, her every word seemed to have led him to the decision at which he'd arrived. She may not know if she loved him, but she didn't want a divorce. That would be too final. Her heart thumping, she dialed Christopher on the home line. It rang until the voicemail kicked in. She didn't leave a message. She called his cell and it went straight to voicemail.

CHAPTER XI

The next three days for Adrianna were difficult. She wasn't able to reach her husband which was the main challenge she was facing. Trey stepped up his attempts to seduce her, but she shut him down every time. Last night they argued because of his wandering hands. He wouldn't keep them to himself on their rides across the island to different Irie Nyam restaurants. Adrianna was tired of fending him off and finally told him point blank that no amount of money—and he was paying her a scandalous amount—would allow her to put up with advances that she didn't want. He shot back that she seemed to want plenty when he picked her up from the airport. He'd caught her unaware and vulnerable, she said. She was beyond that, over him, and in love with her husband. That admission surprised Adrianna when the words flew from her mouth. Shockingly they were true. She didn't understand her about face. But then again she did. She'd woken up at the possible finality of her marriage. In the same way that Christopher had a wake-up call when she lost the baby, she too had one when he talked about ending their marriage. Whatever problem they had, they could work it out. She just had to be willing—both of them had to be.

Trey didn't take her negative without objection. Did her husband make her feel the way he did? Could he satisfy her like he could? All Dri said to that was that her husband was in a different league, and she would not compare the men. She loved her husband, he satisfied her desires, and her moral aberration with Trey wouldn't happen again. He tested her fortitude and kissed her with a familiarity that was embarrassing. Instead of feeling pleasure, Adrianna felt irritated with him for trying to rekindle a flame that she had put out. He was appealing, he was sexy, and he made women want to be in bed with him; but she would no longer be one of them. That lusty spell had lost its charm. She intended to go home and make up with Christopher. Decision made, she told Trey on Wednesday morning that she wanted to change her flight from Friday to that afternoon.

He looked up from his computer and slowly reclined in his chair. His gaze roamed over her face with more than business-like interest. Adrianna shifted in the chair across from him, uncomfortable under the familiarity of his gaze. She smoothed a wrinkle from her Anne Klein black pants and glanced around the room. Waterfall art covered one wall, literally a framed painting with water cascading over rocks on canvass. Trey told her that a thin sheet of glass separated the painting from the battery-powered waterfall. A small container of water at the base of the frame supplied the painting with liquid and kept it going by recycling the supply. Whoever had coordinated the idea was truly creative.

"So you're leaving me?"

Turning her attention to him, she said calmly, "I was never with you, Trey."

"Except for the first day, no," he agreed. "What changed after that first kiss?"

"I told you. I'm married and I'm a Christian."

"You were that when I kissed you." He shrugged in a *so what* type of way.

"I temporarily forgot," she said, feeling remorse return.

"I can make you forget again." His mouth tipped up into a devilish smile that would have made Adrianna succumb to the temptation had she not resolved to resist the pull of her attraction to him.

"I'm sure you could, Trey, but I won't let you," she said softly. "I should have run like Joseph when you tried to kiss me."

"Joseph?" He raised a questioning brow.

"A biblical character who fled from temptation."

"Oh," he said, his eyes turning distant at the mention of the Bible.

He'd been that way ten years ago too, uninterested in

Christianity. She hadn't been interested either. She went to church but lived her life by the world's standards. She'd rediscovered the sweetness of truly walking with God and had gotten re-baptized a while after she miscarried Trey's baby. Adrianna thought of telling him about that loss. He hadn't known she was pregnant then. She was married now and trying to reconcile with her husband. What benefit was there in telling him about the lost child? None.

"I'm glad to hear I'm a temptation."

"Not anymore," she denied.

"Do you want to put it to a test?" he demanded, challenge sparking in his eye.

Adrianna was not stupid. Trey knew how to break down a woman's defenses. He was smooth, charismatic, and persuasive. She was not putting herself into his hands ever again. "No, I don't."

"Scared?" he teased.

"No, just no longer stupid."

He frowned at that. "Kissing me was stupid?"

"And wrong," she added.

"Why did you do it then?"

"Because I was raw and needy and vulnerable."

"And you're not now?" He pitched his voice low, seductive low, and sexy.

"No," she shook her head and met his gaze head on and unflinching.

"I want you. You don't want me. Kind of like poetic justice, isn't it?" He grimaced. "Although, I *did* want you. I just couldn't break the understanding I had with Dahlia. I still want you."

Adrianna glanced away from the heat in his gaze. "You're wealthy and handsome. You can have any woman."

"But not the one I want," he said wryly, watching her with a twisted smile.

"I'm someone else's wife," she reminded him.

"You could be mine. It just takes a little paperwork."

In the same way ten years ago it would have taken only a little paperwork for him to get a divorce, but he had chosen not to. It was her choice now. She looked and him steadily and said, "I love my husband, Trey. I'm not divorcing him."

"You sound like you mean it." He searched her face and saw her seriousness.

"I do."

"So I can't call you if I don't like the final website design or if I have an idea about something I want you to add to the site?"

"Tell Buddy, and he can communicate with me."

"What? Are you scared that you'll fall for me if you hear my voice?" he asked with a grin.

Adrianna laughed because she knew he was joking. "No, it's not that," she denied, turning sober. "But with our history, I think it's best to keep communication to a minimum."

"In case your husband finds out, you mean."

That had run across her mind, but she didn't admit it. "There's really nothing for him to find out."

"Oh. You told him about me then and my baby that you lost."

"You knew about that!" Adrianna gasped.

"Not until a year later. I ran into your friend, Caitlyn, and boy did she give me a good dressing down for leaving you pregnant and all alone to deal with the scandal of being an unwed mother. God, she said, had delivered you from the scandal because you'd had a miscarriage."

Caitlyn was the girl she shared an apartment with in the days when she knew Trey. Her friend never mentioned seeing Trey or speaking with him, probably because she knew Dri had been badly heartbroken when she and he split.

"I'm sorry you lost our baby, Adrianna."

"Would you have claimed it had you known?" She was curious.

"I would have."

"But that would have jeopardized your marriage."

"Dahlia wouldn't have known."

"So he or she would have been a dirty little secret just like me." She said it lightly, feeling nothing now, but it had hurt then that he'd wanted her to be his mistress since he had a wife whom he had no intention of divorcing.

"A secret, yes, but not a dirty one," he said smoothly, making no apologies now just like he hadn't back then for being a married man and sleeping with her.

"I see," she said. It was time to end this conversation. If she intended to catch the six-thirty American Airlines flight out of the MoBay airport, she had to go to the hotel and get her suitcase. She stood and held out her hand. "It's been a pleasure doing business with you, Trey. Thanks for the project. I think you'll like the finished product."

He stood and slowly wrapped his fingers around hers. "I already like what I see," he said. Adrianna had a feeling he wasn't talking about the website sample that she'd worked up over the past few days.

She firmly and swiftly extricated her hand from his. "Good bye, Trey," she said and hurried to the door.

"Adrianna."

She stopped in the doorway and glanced back.

I love you, he mouthed, but with his mischievous smile, she wasn't sure he meant it. She smiled and walked away without another look, pretty much the way he'd left her ten years ago.

CHAPTER XII

Adrianna got home after midnight. She was disappointed when she got to John F. Kennedy airport (JFK) in Queens and found Manuel, Christopher's project manager, waiting for her instead of Christopher. She'd taken pains with her appearance, even courting pneumonia on the plane with the halter she wore just for his benefit. She ended up asking the flight attendant for a blanket to stay warm. Her circulation almost stopped with her skin tight stretch jeans and since they looked sexier than anything with stilettos, she'd donned four inch ones, going for strikingly stunning and hoping to have Christopher panting after her.

Now as she let herself into their split level home, she was tired and irritated. Her feet hurt and she was about to burst out of these pants. She might have to cut herself out of them. Upstairs, she headed straight for her bedroom, and flipped on the light, knowing Christopher wouldn't be there, and froze in shock. In the center of the white comforter was a gigantic heart formed from red rose petals. In the center of that were the words I LOVE YOU, formed from the same petals. Tears springing in her eyes like mini fountains, Adrianna pressed a hand to her madly fluttering heart and covered her mouth with the other. Christopher did this. He loved her, although he hadn't spoken to her since he said he wanted to end their relationship. Oh, Jesus, where was her man? She had to find him in this house and tell him she loved him too. She whirled to head out the door and there he was filling up the doorway, all six feet of bare chocolate muscle save for the Jeans riding low on his hips, unzipped and unbuttoned with nothing beneath.

Like a flash fire, desire flooded her blood, sending SOS messages north and south of her belt line, making places pound and throb with rising need for the man standing there watching her with all the craving she was experiencing outlined on his face. They met halfway, connected like waves crashing into each other. The kiss was fast, sweltering with heat, and urgent with want. Their hands roamed over one another, frenzied touches that sensitized every nerve ending at every point of contact. His body beneath her hands felt firm, and good, and right. No guilt here. He was hers, before the Almighty, to hold and to have, and boy was she doing a lot of that tonight.

When Christopher walked her backwards towards their bed, Adrianna moved with him willingly, more than ready for the loving that lay ahead tonight.

***

One Month Later

Karen stood at the stall door of one of the cubicles in the ladies' room at Selena's watching Adrianna worriedly as her sister heaved and retched over the commode. When Dri finally straightened up and leaned against the wall of the stall, Karen said, "Adrianna, I think you should go see the doctor today."

Adrianna pushed off the wall and flushed. Waving her sister backwards so she could exit the stall, she went to the sink and rinsed her mouth and her face. "Maybe I shouldn't have eaten the Mac and Cheese."

"I was a little shocked when you ordered it. I thought you were off cheese and milk."

"I am but I felt for it." She met her sister's widened eyes in the mirror.

"Felt for it?" Karen repeated, her eyes narrowing speculatively. "Adrianna, are you pregnant?"

Adrianna paused mid-motion in the act of turning off the faucet. Had she missed her period? She didn't know. She hadn't been keeping track. Wracking her brain, trying to remember the last time she had it, her eyes popped. She whipped her phone from her purse and brought up the calendar. Two weeks late! Adrianna turned to Karen. In hushed tones she said, "I'm going to see the doctor."

***

Adrianna stared at the two lines on the pregnancy test stick and didn't know whether to laugh or to weep. Her emotions were on a Kingda Ka type of roller coaster ride. Should she tell Christopher or not? With things between them running smoothly, they had discussed getting pregnant. He was on board whenever she was ready. Dri hadn't gone back to taking birth control. So this pregnancy should come as no surprise. Yesterday she had wanted to go to the doctor, but they didn't have an appointment until this afternoon. Unable to wait that long, she'd bought a test kit at the supermarket. Now it was confirmed. She was pregnant. She would keep her appointment later. Although the doctor had declared her fit on her last visit just before leaving for Jamaica, Adrianna still wondered if she were healthy enough to carry this pregnancy? Was her uterus prepared to hold this baby? She didn't think she could endure another loss.

Holding the stick behind her back, she descended the stairs to find her husband preparing lunch in the kitchen.

"Hey, babe," she called his attention from the bottom step.

He turned and his languorous sweep of admiration made Adrianna feel like an ice cube on a sweltering side walk.

"Good morning, beautiful. How are you?" he asked, walking over and stopping before her.

Adrianna smiled wide and slowly brought her hand forward. "We," she said, "are fine."

Christopher's eyes turned circular and he took the test stick from her with a shaking hand. "You're pregnant?" he asked, his tone full of awe, staring at the two lines in disbelief.

"Yes," she said, laughing and clasping her hands in happiness.

"How do you feel?" Christopher asked, slipping a hand around her waist and pulling her off the step.

"A little nauseated and a bit tired but happy." She looked at him searchingly. "What about you? How do you feel about this?"

He bent and set the test stick on the stairs. Straightening up, he slid his hand beneath her camisole and flattened his palm over her belly. He kissed her and touched his forehead to hers. "You really want to know how I feel?"

"I do," Adrianna smiled.

"I feel," he began, "proud that a part of me is inside of you. I'm looking forward to your waistline expanding with our baby." He tugged her into his embrace and wrapped his arms around her. "And I'm happy that God gave me this second chance."

"Oh, Chris. I love you," Adrianna breathed and kissed him.

He kissed her back. "I'll never tire of hearing you say that, Dri. I love you too."

CHAPTER XIII

Vivene Landry gazed out the first floor bedroom window of Bethany's Bed and Breakfast in the town of Mountain Spring, watching the sunrise make its spectacular appearance. Golden and glistening with a silver lining, the sun rose to grace the morning as darkness gave way and dawn emerged.

Located on one of the back roads, the B and B sat at the end of the street atop a hill. The sunset last evening had been breathtaking. An explosion of orange colored the evening sky, edging out tufts of clouds and the soft grey-blue hue of the heavens. In some places, long melon-tinged strips crisscrossed belts of indigo as night claimed the skies. Beautiful. There was no other way to put it.

Letting the drapes fall back in place, she glanced at her watch and then towards the bed. A dark head with neat cornrows reclined on the pillow on the left side of the double bed. The five year old shifted and rolled to her back. Her small mouth parted slightly as she breathed. Her curly black lashes resembled curved rows of snarled wire. Her short nose with flattened bridge made her the cutest little person in the world, at least in her mother's mind as she gazed lovingly at her daughter. Relaxed in sleep, she was the picture of innocence. If Emily didn't get up soon, she'd miss the buffet breakfast. The muffins were homemade and exceptional, not the usual store brand. She'd enjoyed them yesterday. Thought of time reminded Vivene of her reason for coming to Mountain Spring. She'd been procrastinating and the clock was ticking. She'd taken seven days leave from her job to do this. She was into the third day of this journey and she had yet to contact the man she'd come to this town to see. Vivene took another look at the caramel colored child, her complexion a cross between Vivene's butterscotch skin and her father's chocolate one. For Emily's sake she had to make contact and get this over with.

***

Christopher barely spent time in his office, which was a miniscule square footage of space with a receptionist/word processor/bookkeeper. Large pictures of his recent jobs graced the walls and plants occupied what limited space that filing cabinets, water cooler and Carol's desk and chair didn't take up. This morning he ran in to screen the letters she had prepared for his signature and to drop off the thumb drive with some additional promotional materials for the fall season, which Adrianna had done the layout for. Carol just had to print them.

Rushing out the door, he threw some last minute instructions at Carol, swung around and knocked a woman backwards who had been coming in the door. Reacting fast, he grabbed for her, catching the strap on her summer dress and the strap of her bra. He hauled her forward and apologized, "I'm so sorry. Are you okay?"

She looked up and Christopher stared in shock. "Vivene!" He hadn't seen her in what? Five or six years. What was she doing here?

"Hi, Christopher," she murmured, her smile a bit shaky. "How are you?"

"Great," he said and asked, his brows knitted, "Are you sure you're okay?"

"I'm fine," she assured him.

He released her, chalking up her trembling to the scare of nearly falling. "It's been a long time," he observed and then regretted the thoughtless remark when she blushed, remembering as she no doubt did, the last time they were together. One dark night, two lonely people, and it didn't take rocket science to figure out what happened. They hadn't repeated it and parted amicably. Christopher cleared his throat, "How are you? And what brings you to Mountain Spring?"

She moistened already glossy lips. Christopher figured she was nervous, although he didn't know why.

"I'm fine," she said answering his first question. "As to what brings me to Mountain Spring..." Her voice faded and she looked down before finishing with a low shocker. "You."

"Me?" he echoed, sure he'd heard wrong. "I don't understand." He frowned in bewilderment at her.

She looked behind him to gossip girl, Carol, whom he could imagine was straining her ears.

"Is there someplace private where we can talk?" She whispered.

He stepped out onto the sidewalk and closed the door. People were passing on the street, but not many. This was as private as it was going to get. He looked at his watch. He had twenty minutes to make it to his nine thirty appointment. He had a referral from a current client. Someone in the Estate Hills area of Mohawk Valley wanted an indoor winter garden where they could entertain throughout the cold while maintaining the illusion of summer. He had some ideas from the initial phone consultation, but needed to see the area he would be working with. Vivene had to talk fast. He couldn't be late. "I've got an appointment in twenty minutes, Vivene. Can you make it quick? Sorry for the rush. I don't mean to be rude." He smiled to support the sincerity of his words.

She glanced from him to the white Nissan Altima parked next to the pavement a few feet from them. She'd been doing that quite a bit in the less than five minutes of their re-acquaintance. "Come with me please," she requested and moved to the vehicle. Curious, Christopher followed her. She opened the rear right passenger door and a little girl with thick shiny twists falling to her shoulders stepped out. Caramel brown and dressed in a lilac T-shirt, Jeans, and what looked like Hello Kitty sneakers, she looked cute. When she looked up with a more gum than teeth smile, Christopher thought her adorable.

"Christopher, please meet Emily, my daughter...and yours."

He felt like he'd been slapped hard. Still trying to get his bearings, he shook his head. "Repeat that, please."

Vivene attempted a smile but her lips trembled and fell short of it. "Emily's yours. When we were together that time, I conceived. You're looking at the result of it." The words tumbled out in a rush as if she thought he would interrupt her.

Christopher did, but with a raised hand because he was fighting to find a response to all he was hearing. "I thought you said," he started, and then stopped and pitched his voice lower at Emily's interested stare. "I thought you said your tubes were tied," he whispered.

"They were," she whispered back, paused, and then added, "just not at the time."

Christopher stared at her nonplussed. So she had lied? He closed his eyes and ran a hand over his head. Why was he afflicted with women who couldn't tell the truth where procreation was concerned? He opened his eyes as he thought of something else. If she'd lied about that, was she telling the truth that this girl was his? "I'll need DNA testing done," he said, leveling a no-nonsense stare at her.

She nodded. "I expected that. I went to a local lab here in town and all three of us need to have blood samples or buccal swabs done to be sent off-site."

"Buccal swabs?"

"A mouth swab. You know like when the doctor wipes cotton on the inside of your cheek to get a tissue sample."

"How long does it take to get the results?" He asked because she seemed to know more than he did about this type of testing. Frankly all he knew of it was that men could use it to definitively know if a child was theirs.

"Three to ten business days."

"Today is Tuesday, so we wouldn't get results until the middle or end of next week."

"Right. So we have to do it today."

He glanced at his watch again. If he didn't move, he'd be more than ten minutes late for his appointment. He needed to call Mrs. Pearson, but he needed to talk to Vivene as well. If this child were indeed his, why had she waited until now to tell him? What did she want? Did she even realize he was married? Christopher didn't want to think about how Adrianna would react or what she would think. True, this was an indiscretion before he came to church and before he married her, but no wife wanted to be faced with the evidence of a husband's interaction with another woman. Maybe he wouldn't have to tell Adrianna anything. Maybe the test would prove that he wasn't the father. He looked at his watch again and made a quick decision. "Vivene, leave your car here and come with me, you and Emily. I have an appointment, and we need to talk. We can do it on the ride to Mohawk Valley."

"What about the testing?" she asked as she locked her car doors and followed him to his Dodge Pick up truck.

"We won't do it here," he said tersely, opening the front passenger door for her and the rear for Emily. It was a small town, and his church community was even smaller. He didn't want to do a test like that in a place where someone might know him. Despite patient confidentiality, things leaked and he didn't want anybody hearing he might have fathered a child and start running conjectures about whether he'd stepped out on Dri. Stories got twisted in the retelling and sometimes from the get go. He slammed both doors and walked around the truck's hood, dialing Mrs. Pearson as he went.

CHAPTER XIV

As he flew down Highway one, Christopher shot questions at the woman who was holding onto the handle of the door as if she feared an accident were imminent. With his speed, he wasn't surprised.

"Why did you wait until now to tell me about her?" he asked, jerking his head in Emily's direction.

"I never planned to tell you. I got saved three months ago, and it's been on my conscience ever since. I didn't think it was fair to Emily to grow up without a father, and I couldn't live the lie anymore that I didn't know where you were."

She was a Christian? "So you had a revelation?"

"No, more like a chastisement from the Holy Spirit. It pressed on me so heavily that I told Emily that I'd lied, that she had a father, and that he was in another state."

"Where do you live now?"

"Nevada."

Clear across the country. Visitation would be tricky. If she's yours, he told himself.

"Did Alexandra know about the pregnancy?"

His sister, Alex, was the one who'd introduced them. He'd gone to visit her a year after Cindy died. Vivene had lived in the apartment above Alex's.

"She did, but of course not that it was yours."

"And it never crossed your mind that I would want to know."

"I was the one who wanted a baby. With nobody permanent in my life, I decided to get what I wanted and raise my child alone."

Christopher gritted his teeth and gripped the wheel. Déjà vu. Adrianna all over again. He shut the bitter thought down. He and his wife were past that. But this, what Vivene just admitted to doing, was a mirror image of Dri's duplicity. "So you lied about the tubal ligation?"

"I did," she said in a small voice and had the decency to sound ashamed. "Can you slow down a bit?" she asked, her voice uncertain.

Christopher eased off the gas. He hadn't realized he was doing ninety. "What do you expect from me if it turns out she's mine?"

"I don't want anything, not even support. I don't need it. I make good money and can provide for her."

"If not financial, what is it?"

"Just be the dad that she's always wanted," she said softly. "One like all the other kids have. One who shows up at school functions at least sometimes, one who tells her that he loves her, one who makes time for her."

"I live across the country, Vivene. How do you expect me to do that?"

"I could move here."

Christopher sighed heavily. The situation moved from bad to worse with her statement. "Vivene, I'm married."

"I wouldn't be a problem to you and your wife," she rushed to reassure him.

He slid her a get real glance. He couldn't deal with Emily and not with her, and inevitably, at some point, Dri would have to. "Don't rush to do that—move here—just yet," he cautioned. One thing at a time. Paternity test and then action if necessary.

***

Adrianna had spent the day in Heart Haven. Her plan to go back to Mountain Spring for her Genetiks Lab appointment derailed when she looked at the time. She wouldn't make it. Scrolling the internet via her phone, she found a Genetiks Lab in downtown Heart Haven. Her doctor had given her a prescription for blood work, which she should have done two days ago, but hadn't gotten around to. Another day would go by if she tried to make it to Mountain Spring.

She maneuvered the Nissan Sentra into a parking spot and walked into the lab. Making fast work of the lengthy paperwork, she sat down and prepared to wait. A nurse came quickly and called her in. Adrianna followed the woman down the wide corridor. The white doors on either side created an aura of peace and calm in a place full of pain, what with all the needle pricks people endured in a lab. The woman took her vitals and told her the phlebotomist would be in shortly to draw her blood.

***

"I thought they were going to stick me with a needle," Emily said, sounding relieved.

Christopher smiled down at the little girl as he, she, and her mother exited the examination room where they'd all given DNA samples. He squeezed the hand she'd placed in his from the time they entered the exam room. His heart compressed with a funny little feeling at the trust contained in the gesture. Deep in his head he felt like he wouldn't mind if she were his. He slid his thoughts from that idea. She had gotten nervous when the phlebotomist entered the room and refused to have her cheek swabbed first, thinking that it would hurt. Christopher stepped up to have his done, demonstrating the painlessness of it. From that point he became her hero. She took his hand in a firm grip and opened her mouth willingly to be buccal swabbed.

"It didn't hurt at all," the child continued, skipping to keep up with Christopher's longer strides.

He shortened his steps. "I told you it wouldn't," he said.

"I'm glad you're my daddy."

The unexpected statement stopped Christopher dead in his tracks.

"Emily!" Vivene exclaimed.

Christopher looked from the girl to her mother. He raised an eyebrow. When had she explained this whole process to the child and what exactly had she told her?

"She's smart. I had to explain who you were."

Christopher shot a quick look up and down the corridor and controlled a spurt of annoyance. It was empty. Thank God. "You told her I'm her dad?" he muttered beneath his breath. She was that sure he was Emily's father?

"I had to," she said, looking at him helplessly, her brown eyes pleading for understanding, pleading for him not to deny it or contradict her.

He looked down at Emily, and his heart melted at her endearing smile. For her sake, he kept his peace. "We'll talk later," he told Vivene.

***

Adrianna clutched the handle of the door to keep from keeling over. Lifting a shaking hand to cover her mouth, she stifled the sound of anguish as her tears fell and shook her head in attempted silent denial of what she'd just heard. *I'm glad you are my daddy.* The words replayed in her head, establishing the reality she was trying not to believe. Christopher had a child he had never told her about. With how tiny the girl was from the rear view, she couldn't be more than four or five. Did that mean the child had been born while they were dating? Oh, dear Lord Jesus! He'd cheated on her, and with the woman and child's presence, it seemed like he was still doing that. She'd been about to step out of the room to find the ladies' room when she heard his voice. About to call out to him, the sight of him walking with a strange woman and child, with the girl's hand encased in his, killed any plan to speak to him. Too shocked, she watched them walk away while her mind careened all over the place, grappling with the implications of what she'd just seen and heard.

CHAPTER XV

Trouble travels in pairs. That statement became true for Christopher when he got home that evening. As if the possibility of fatherhood wasn't enough to worry about, what he discovered in the mail made him wish letters hadn't been delivered to his address today. Adrianna wasn't home, which was a good thing because he would have ended up in jail.

He sat on the sofa in their living room, staring at the frozen frame of his television's screen. The more he looked at the picture, the more enraged he became. Needing an outlet for the fury he was feeling, he pushed off the sofa, and strode to the rear of the house. Shoving the rear doors of the den open, he stormed into his back yard and kicked over one of the patio chairs. It didn't help. He wanted to bellow at the evidence of Adrianna's infidelity. Since he couldn't he vented mentally. Jesuuuuuuuuus! A business trip she'd said. What a bold faced lie. Adrianna hadn't gone to Jamaica on business. It was more like pleasure—very personal, promiscuous pleasure from what he'd seen on the screen. Christopher had no idea who had sent him that DVD recording of his wife making out, to put it mildly, with some man called, Trey. What made him see red even more was the fact that Trey was the one she'd mistaken him for when she'd woken up in the hospital after the miscarriage. At the time he thought she'd been disoriented from the drugs and was talking incoherently. Apparently, she'd been calling for this man. How long had she been carrying on with him? Who was he?

Christopher placed his hands atop his head. *Oh, Jesus, why did I pick up the mail today?* He had only opened the package because he'd been researching vacation spots, wanting to surprise his unfaithful wife with a trip. He thought the package was from one of the resorts he'd made inquiries about. When he'd called her in Jamaica, she'd said she felt nothing for him. Now he knew it was because all her feelings had been channeled towards this man. His heart began pounding as he came to a sudden realization. Based on the doctor's calculations, Adrianna had conceived about the time she returned from Jamaica. That meant this baby might not even be his!

***

Adrianna unlocked the door, cringing as the lock clicked. It was late, after nine. After she left the lab, she hadn't gone home, not wanting to face Christopher. She still didn't want to do that, not yet anyway. She was struggling to accept what she had seen and heard. One side of her brain denied it while the other pounded her to accept the reality of what she had seen and overheard. Now as she opened the door and saw Christopher asleep on the sofa, relief eddied through her, and she started tiptoeing past him to the stairs.

"You're sneaking in here in the same way you were sneaking around with another man behind my back."

Christopher's words froze Adrianna in her tracks. He wasn't asleep! He was just pretending! All she'd seen earlier rushed with the blood to her head and colored her vision red. This scheming, double-dealing piece of trash had the gall to accuse her of his sin, his crime, his chicanery. What foolishness was he spouting about her seeing another man? In high dudgeon, she whirled and let loose like an automatic rifle. "Just look who is talking. You have the audacity to talk to me about seeing somebody when you've stepped out on me, have a child, and are still having an affair!" She glared at him lying there on the sofa looking shocked. "Umm. Didn't know I knew, did you?"

"How do you know?"

It was Dri's turn to stare in disbelief now. He wasn't going to deny it? He wasn't going to dispel her accusation? He didn't have the decency or the consideration to at least try that? "You are really despicable. You know that?" She gave him a disgusted look. "How long has this been going on?" she demanded. "How long have you been sleeping with her? God, it must have been a long time if you've got a child by her." Adrianna laughed mirthlessly and shook her head.

"She's not mine," he denied tightly.

"Now, you're going to deny it!" Adrianna raised her voice. "Now after you all but said she's yours."

"I'm not sure she's mine," he amended with a scowl. Swinging his legs to the floor, he sat up and then stood.

"Oh, now you're not sure when a minute ago you claimed her," Adrianna derided, her hands settling on her hips in combat mode. "She called you daddy and she's not yours." She raked him from top to toe with a disparaging glance. "I wasn't born yesterday, Christopher," she said scornfully.

He watched her steadily for a while, his expression unreadable. Finally, he said, "I'm going to explain something to you. Whether or not you believe me is entirely up to you. If you heard that girl call me daddy, then you must have been at Genetik's lab in Heart Haven earlier."

She nodded in response to his raised right brow.

"The little girl's name is Emily and her mother is Vivene. A year after Cindy died I met her. Both of us were lonely. It was a one-time thing. Today, she came to me to let me know that Emily was mine and she wanted me to get to know her."

"After six years?" Adrianna raised a skeptical eyebrow.

"She said she'd gotten saved a—"

Adrianna snorted at the 'saved' bit.

"I wouldn't ridicule her if I were you," her husband warned, his voice turning cold and his gaze hostile.

Dri was taken aback. Why was he being antagonistic just because she scoffed at a woman whom he claimed he'd known once years ago? Did this so called, Vivene, mean more to him than he was saying?

"Now," he went on, "she says she accepted Christ and no longer wants to withhold Emily's existence from me because she thought it the right thing to do. Emily's been asking about her father and Vivene didn't want to deceive her anymore. We were at the clinic taking samples for DNA testing. I want to make sure she's mine."

"And if she is?" Adrianna loved kids, but she had ambivalent feelings about accepting a child her husband had by another woman.

"I'll do what's right by her." He shrugged as if there was nothing else to it.

"And what exactly does that mean?"

"I'll support her financially and be as much a part of her life as I can be."

Adrianna didn't like the sound of that at all. "I'm not comfortable with that," she stated, making her feelings plain from the get go.

"You don't have to be. If I'm her father, I have to do what's right by her."

His flat, *you-have-no-say-so* tone lit Dri's temper. "*You* have to do right by her! *You!*" She flashed. "Everything you do affects me and vice versa. So if you're going to do what's right by her by supporting her with time and money, it affects me and our family. You forget that you have a child on the way." She placed a hand on her two month belly. "The time you spend with that little girl will take time away from this baby. The money you spend on her means there's less for this baby and this family. I'm not saying that you shouldn't take care of her, but before you make any decision to do so, you need to talk to me and *we* need to decide together how to handle this. This is not a solo effort, Christopher. This, what we have," she waved her hand back and forth between them, "is a union. "

The last word was barely out of her mouth when his voice hit her like whiplash. "You prostituted yourself with another man, made yourself his whore, and have the audacity to call this marriage a union!" he thundered.

Adrianna jumped at his octave and recoiled from his word choice. She stepped back until she hit the living room's wall as he advanced and her heart pumped with fright at the violence in his face. "Wh-what are you talking about?" she asked shakily.

"I am talking about your lying," he hissed. "I am talking about your cheating," he gritted. "I am talking about your ADULTERY WITH TREY."

Oh, God! Oh, God! He knew about Trey? What? How? When? The questions tumbled around in her head like tennis balls in a game of doubles. Shaking with fear and guilt, she tried to speak but couldn't form words. Her husband gave her a look so full of loathing that if she could, Adrianna would have folded into herself to escape the abhorrence in his eyes.

"Your business trip to Jamaica wasn't one. You went to be with that man, same one you thought was holding you at the hospital when you miscarried."

Same one who was holding her at the hospital? What was he talking about?

"You called his name when I held you at the hospital," Christopher said bitterly. "You opened your eyes and called me 'Trey.' I didn't put things together until I watched the DVD this afternoon."

Adrianna's heart nearly flew out of her chest. "DVD?" she asked, her voice hushed and filled with trepidation.

He spun around and snatched the remote from the central table. One point and click and Adrianna watched her life going down the drain in living color. Right there on the TV's screen she watched herself and Trey in an amorous embrace in the rear seat of the limo she'd ridden in from the Montego Bay airport. How had Christopher gotten this? Who had recorded them? Trey? But to what intent? Was he that desperate to have her that he'd done this to wreck her marriage? If he loved her like he said he did, he wouldn't have done this. If not him, who? How could she ever explain what she was watching on the screen? How could she convince her husband that it was a momentary slip in judgment? After seeing this, no wonder Christopher believed that she'd slept with Trey. The screen went suddenly black, and the remote hit the TV screen with a crack. Adrianna flinched and watched it bounce to the hardwood floor with a thud and slide across wood with a swish.

The room was silent. Adrianna was afraid to look at Christopher. She leaned against the wall, kept her eyes on the floor and trembled.

"Is that the reason you ran into my arms so eagerly the night you came back from Jamaica? Is it that you were trying to cover the evidence of your unfaithfulness? Well now you can't, and there is nothing that will make me believe the child you're carrying is mine."

Adrianna jerked her head up then, and the cold intent in her husband's face made her believe what he'd said. "C-Chris, th-this is your baby. I-I didn't sleep with him."

"You really think I believe that after what we just saw?" He gave her a pitying glance. "I may be blind a bit where you're concerned, but I'm no fool. You're not going to saddle me with that man's baby."

Her already unsteady heartbeat slipped even more. He said nothing would make him believe that this baby was his, but she had to convince him. This was a war that she had to win. She stepped away from the wall and approached him with cautious steps. Stopping an arm's length away from him, she spoke, "C-Chris, I wish you'd never seen that."

"Really." He said scornfully. "You wished I'd been in the dark but not that you never gave your body to another man."

Adrianna closed her eyes briefly. "I didn't sleep with him," she repeated her earlier statement. Now would not be the time to tell him she once had.

"His hands were all over you and his tongue down your throat. Like a dog in heat you welcomed him. You didn't try to stop him which tells me you wanted it as much as he did."

Tears stinging her eyes, Adrianna kept shaking her head denying the undeniable, struggling for words to dispute her husband's accusations and unable to come up with any. "I didn't mean to do it," she whispered.

"Didn't mean to do it!" he roared. "What? You lost your freaking mind? Had temporary insanity? What?"

Adrianna hugged herself, trying to stop the shaking. She had no answers but she had to try. Oh, God, why had she ever run across Trey again? "Trey—"

"Trey?"

Adrianna realized her slip the same time he did. When she shot a fast look at Chris, the menace in his expression didn't bode well for her. "Chris, I meant t—"

"Shut your mouth! Or so help me I'll shut it for you!"

With his hand raised and ready for a blow it seemed, Adrianna believed him. She took a cautious step backwards and he advanced. Dreading what he might do, she turned to flee upstairs, but he caught her arm in a grip so bruising that Adrianna cried out.

He shoved her against the wall and wrapped his fingers around her neck. Her eyes widening with terror, Adrianna grabbed for his hand, trying to pry his fingers from around her throat. His grip only got tighter. Oh God, he truly meant to strangle her! Tears running fast and steady down her face like a pipe with a washer gone bad she pleaded even though he'd warned her to keep silent, "P-Please, Chris. D-Don't do this. I-I know how you feel."

"NO YOU DON'T!" He bellowed—each emphasized word like a shrinking noose, cutting off her air supply as his fingers tightened around her neck with each enunciation. Choking, she scrabbled desperately at his hand, fighting for fast dwindling oxygen and praying for salvation. Her vision blurred and the room began to swim out of focus. Suddenly, as if he realized what he was doing, Christopher's fingers slackened. Coughs wracked Dri's frame as air charged into her burning lungs. Beneath the sawing sound of her labored breathing, she heard him say, "You don't know how I feel." His words, barely a whisper this time, came out in such tortured tones, that Adrianna wiped her eyes to get a clear look at him. Her heart splintered at the pain in his face. She had hurt him, she knew; but the depth of the anguish in his eyes and the magnitude of the torment on his face made her wish she could turn the clock back and erase her act of sin. Closing her eyes she silently begged, Oh, Lord Jesus, please forgive me and please, please, God, please fix my marriage.

"You don't know how it feels to watch another man touch my wife here," he placed his hand on her belly, "and here," he shifted to her hip, "and here," he slid his hand down her thigh, "and most of all here," he touched her lips.

Adrianna opened her eyes then, and her heart, what was left of it, shattered when she saw the tears in Christopher's eyes and the teardrops slipping down his cheeks.

"You were mine to touch and to taste and to hold, only mine, and you let him take that away from me. You let him steal our intimacy just hours after you left me without a kiss, an embrace, or a soft word. And then you permitted him the ultimate liberty and let him destroy our union by giving him access here." He touched her in her most intimate place, and Adrianna started crying again because she knew she would never be able to convince her husband that the last part of his statement wasn't true. The evidence of all her indiscretions was too overwhelming for him to draw any conclusion different from what he did.

She had let Trey steal everything, Chris had said—everything except her heart. "Christopher," she whispered softly, "I love you."

He watched her for a long time, a bittersweet smile twisting his lips. "I wish I could tell you I didn't love you, but I'd be lying. Right now though, Dri, I hate you more than I love you." He released her, stepped away, and walked out the front door, closing it quietly behind him.

CHAPTER XVI

"K-Karen, p-pick up please."

Karen stilled her husband's wandering hands at the shaky, watery sound of her sister's voice leaving a message on the answering machine.

"Call her later," Douglas whispered, distracting her with a trail of hot kisses from her collarbone to her chest and all places nearby.

She almost yielded to his persuasion when her sister started sobbing. "Something's wrong," she said worriedly, pushing out of his arms and leaving him behind. Douglas ground his teeth in frustration and thought that family far or near could be a trial and a cross.

"Hi, Dri. What's going on?"

Karen listened quietly as the whole story poured out between tears, sniffles, and blows. "Dri, I really don't know what to say, and even more I don't know what to do. This has so many snarls in it that I don't know where to begin unraveling it." She glanced over her shoulder at her husband at Adrianna's question.

Douglas raised an eyebrow.

"Did Christopher come over earlier tonight while I was out?"

He shook his head.

"No, Dri. Douglas didn't see him tonight. What? You want Douglas to call him? Do you think he'll answer even though he didn't answer any of your calls? Okay, okay, Dri. Take it easy. I get it. You don't know what else to do. I'll have Douglas call him."

Karen disconnected the line and turned around to face her

husband's *don't-drag-me-into-this* stare. She gave him a *honey-please-do-this* look.

"What is it?" he asked, sighing in resignation.

She explained what Adrianna had told her about the fight and the reasons for it.

Douglas looked at his watch when his wife finished talking. It was nearly midnight. "If he does pick up the call, what am I to say? What explanation shall I give for calling him at this time of the night?" he asked Karen.

She frowned at him. "You're an eloquent preacher. Pick some words that make sense out of your extensive vocabulary and come up with a reason for calling him."

"You know, if I didn't know you to be my sweet, mostly even-tempered wife, I'd think you were getting sarcastic with me," he said mildly with a slight smile.

Karen leaned forward and gave him a quick kiss. "Sorry dear," she said, sincere now. Placing the phone in his hand she promised, "I'll make it up to you later."

He slid his hand over her belly and would have gone further if she hadn't stopped him. "Behave," Karen giggled. "Let's help Adrianna and Christopher and then I'll take care of you."

"I'll hold you to it," he warned and dialed his brother-in-law.

***

Christopher glanced at his phone's screen when it rang and let it continue ringing when he recognized the number. His in-laws were calling. No doubt Adrianna had called her sister and she in turn was calling him. He didn't want to talk to her. Why would she think he'd want to talk to her relatives? Settling more comfortably against the pillows of the queen sized bed in the room he'd secured for the next two days in a local hotel, he closed his eyes and tried not to think about his wife or what she had done.

Next he heard the cash register tone he'd set for an incoming text. They were texting him now like she had after the calling failed. He hadn't read her text after the first one. He'd do the same with his in-laws. Christopher tapped the screen of his phone and read the message: *Chris, it's Doug. Where are you? It's after midnight. I want to sleep and your wife and my wife aren't letting me. They want to know if you're okay. Please don't tell me where you are. They'll make me come there or worse come bother you. Do me a favor, text me to say you're alive.*

84

Christopher grinned despite his problems. His brother in law was funny—smart and shrewd too. He texted back to say he was alive. The phone went quiet after that. Christopher supposed his answer satisfied them. He wished a simple text message could fix the problem between him and Dri. He wished she hadn't cheated on him. He wished he hadn't seen the DVD. Since life was complicated and he was living it, simple wasn't possible.

How long had she been seeing this man? Had the first pregnancy even been his? Had he done something wrong to make her want somebody else? Why would she let another man put his hands on her? Jesus, when he thought about it, he felt sick. The anger was gone and all that remained was bitter disappointment. He'd never in a million years thought she would commit adultery. The Bible preached forgiveness innumerable times and talked about Moses mentioning divorce because of the hardness of men's hearts and their unwillingness to reconcile differences. How did you reconcile something like this though? The thought of making love with Adrianna now, knowing that another man had touched territory that had been exclusively his for two years repelled him. If it had been before they met, he could forgive that, but post marriage and with what he'd seen, Christopher knew he couldn't. The images were with him for life, condemning her, declaring her guilty forever.

***

Christopher groaned and buried his head deeper under his pillow. His phone was ringing again. He'd meant to put it on vibrate, but he must have fallen asleep. The lamp on the night stand was still on. The digital clock showed two a.m. as the time. Sighing, he reached for the phone the same time it got silent. Douglas again. This time he'd called from his cell phone. The ka-ching sound of an incoming text went off again. Christopher checked the message: *Hey. Doug again. R u sleeping or ignoring me? It's quiet over here. Girls r asleep. Karen made me go get Dri. Said it wasn't safe for her to be alone when she was so distraught.*

Christopher felt a spurt of annoyance at that. What was she distressed about? That she'd been found out? That he'd walked out? What did she expect after what he had seen? He read the rest of Douglas's message: *If you want to talk, now's a good time. We can talk, text, or I can come over. Won't give your location away. Promise—on the Bible if you want me to.*

Christopher knew he could trust Douglas. Somehow though, he had reservations about admitting to anybody that his wife had had an affair. It made him feel like he was inadequate, that he had come up short in some way, that he hadn't been able to fulfill her needs so she'd run to another man. He texted the address to Douglas.

CHAPTER XVII

Douglas drove through the streets of downtown Mountain Spring in the early hours of the cold November morning headed for The Quiet Inn in the Southeast corner of town. Like in the suburbs, nothing moved or stirred, not even the scanty leaves on the several maple and birch trees common to the area. Silence blanketed downtown and darkness covered some blocks of Main Street. The town board, in a budget saving measure, had voted to turn off the street lights on every other block during the night.

Putting on his right signal, he turned unto Beauford Street and made a right into the Inn's parking lot. Doors were locked at midnight. He called Christopher to let him in.

***

Douglas sat on the single swivel chair in his brother-in-law's hotel room and listened while the man talked. He was raw with hurt and disillusioned with a marriage he thought was working just fine after the last obstacle he and Adrianna had overcome. Now he knew for sure that he didn't have a marriage because he couldn't get past what Adrianna had done.

"Are you saying then that you don't love her?" Douglas asked when he finished.

"That's the hard part. I love her, but I abhor what she's done."

"But you don't despise her."

"Right now, Doug, I hate her."

"Humm," Douglas said, hearing what the other man wasn't

87

saying. He didn't hear the venomous stress on the word 'hate' that he'd been expecting. There was room for hope here. Right now his brother-in-law was hurting and he could imagine that seeing his wife invoked revulsion, yet he loved her still.

"Did you ever consider that she might be telling the truth?"

"You mean that she hadn't slept with him?"

"Yes."

Christopher looked at him as if he were nuts. "Douglas the man had his hands all over her. He was kissing her beyond French connection, and you want me to believe they didn't go the whole nine yards?" Christopher's expression said, *you can believe that if you want but I'm not that stupid.* "Besides, it isn't just that making me not trust her. Her infidelity isn't the only reason why I don't believe her. She lied about taking birth control pills when she wasn't. We got past that and now this happened."

"I get that it's hard to believe something in the face of contrary evidence, Chris. I understand. I was where you are once with my wife. She built our friendship on lies and deceit and married me just to get even with my parents. Pregnancy and job loss were the only things that brought her back to me. I'm sure you've heard some if not all the story from one or both of the girls."

He nodded.

"But here we are three years later very much happy and in love. It was a struggle, an extreme one for me, but I got to the place where I hurt more being separated from my wife than I did being with her. Like in your situation, she apologized for everything she did wrong and then something else cropped up to put another wedge between us. Only to find out later that that wedge had been deliberately built to hurt my wife and for me to believe she was still lying to me and was untrustworthy. Have you thought about where this DVD came from? Who sent it? What was their intent? Was it to drive a wedge between you and Dri?"

"I've thought about all that, but it doesn't negate the fact that she's the one on it making love with this guy. How do you explain that away?"

"You don't. You forgive it."

"Are you out of your mind?" Christopher considered his brother-in-law and wondered which part of the earth he came from. Shifting closer to the edge of the bed on which he was seated, he struck his fist against his palm, emphasizing the points he was making. "Do you have any idea how embarrassing it is to see another man doing to your wife what only you are supposed to do? Do you know how humiliating it is to think that she'd gone somewhere else to get love because you couldn't satisfy her? Can you imagine how hurtful it is to know that she let somebody rob you of the sacredness of the intimacy God gave to only you and her?"

"I can't know all those things unless like they say, I walk a mile in your shoes, Christopher. What I can tell you is that I can relate. When Karen left me on our wedding night, I had to go back to our church alone when the people were expecting a couple to return. I had to tell the board of elders that my wife wouldn't be coming because she'd changed her mind about wanting to be married. They all thought she'd left me because I didn't satisfy her. As if coming home married and without a wife wasn't enough, I had to face the pity and the embarrassment of people thinking I didn't know how to make love to my wife. You can imagine how much I hated her by the time she came back. Yet underneath the hatred, my heart wouldn't let go of the love that made me marry her in the first place.

"I think you're in the same place with Adrianna, Christopher. By admission, you hate her right now but you haven't stopped loving her. You need to talk to your wife and find out what was going through her mind when she let another man touch her. I had to talk with Karen to try to understand what was going on in her mind that motivated her to punish me for something my parents had done over twenty years ago. Honestly, to this day I don't fully understand how she did what she did. But I made a decision, both of us made the decision, to let go of the past and not to allow it to eclipse our future.

"When you talk with Adrianna, you might never understand why she did what she did, but both of you will have to come to the place where you say what's done is done and we're moving forward from here together in Christ. The alternative is separation and as Christians, it's not an option we want to embrace."

Christopher closed his eyes and let Douglas's words wash over him. His in-law made a lot of sense. His head told him that, but his heart was hurting too much for him to accept it right now. As if he sensed the struggle in the silence, Douglas offered, "Let me pray with you, Chris."

"I don't want to pray right now, Doug," he confessed hoarsely, clearing the lump forming in his throat from the quagmire of problems his life had become in mere hours.

"That's all right. You don't have to say a thing. I'll do all the talking."

Christopher bowed his head as the other man rested his hand on his shoulder.

"Dear Lord, we thank You for life and for giving it to us in abundance. In this world we'll have trouble but we thank You that You, our Perfect Example, have overcome the world. Right now, God, we present Christopher before You and ask that You will calm the turmoil in his mind. He's raw, he's in pain, and he's hurting really badly, Jesus. We ask that You will give him the comfort that he desperately needs right now, the peace that passes human understanding that only You can give. Lord there is no problem that You cannot solve and no relationship that You cannot fix. However, our human hearts sometimes resist Your voice. I'm asking You to allow Christopher to hear Your voice so he can know how to proceed with his relationship. I'm asking You speak to Adrianna that she too can hear You and obey Your instruction. Lord, at the end of the day, I ask for healing for both their hearts and pray that a spirit of forgiveness will be exhibited in this marriage. In the final analysis, Lord, please save this marriage to the glory of Your name. This is my prayer in Jesus name. Amen." He squeezed Christopher's shoulders as the man wept and wiped more than a few tears from his own eyes. When his brother in law reached up and squeezed the hand on his shoulder, Douglas understood that it was his way of saying thank you without words.

CHAPTER XVIII

Adrianna flew to the doctor's office the next morning in a panic. She got up this morning to find spotting on her liner. Karen had to calm her down and tell her that it didn't mean she was losing the baby and that this sometimes happened to pregnant women. It had happened to her. While Adrianna quieted, she didn't believe her sister. Something was wrong with her. Her womb was rejecting the baby just like it had two times before. God was punishing her for her wickedness. Karen told her to stop talking nonsense.

After the examination, the doctor asked her a few questions.

"Have you done any heavy lifting lately?"

Adrianna shook her head.

"Has anything changed in your physical activity?"

"What do you mean?" Adrianna raised quizzical brows.

"You haven't been using elliptical machines or lifting weights at the gym for example, have you?"

"No."

"How about your stress levels?"

Since last night it had been through the roof. She'd been wondering if the bleeding had anything to do with that. "It has been a little high of late?"

"Super high or just mild."

"Super," Adrianna admitted with downcast eyes, wondering what the woman would think if she told her about the night she'd had.

"Well, there's our culprit. We've got to get rid of that stress to prevent recurrence of this. Try not to let things bother you. Step back or walk away. Remember it's not just your health now, but hers or his as well."

"Okay, Dr. Island. I'll try to remember that."

"I'll see you in two weeks then," she said with a smile.

***

Adrianna called Christopher again, about the tenth time since she'd woken up this morning. She texted him about the same number of times. Desperate she texted, *I went to the doctor this morning.* The immediate reply she expected didn't come. Sighing, Adrianna looked at her phone and made one more call.

***

"I'm really sorry to hear what happened, Adrianna, but I didn't do that. I feel bad that you thought that I would." He sounded hurt, and Dri felt badly herself. "I do know who did it though."

"You do? Who?"

"My driver or I should say my ex-driver."

"Sammy?" She was taken aback. He'd seemed like such a nice man.

"Yeah, Sammy." Trey sounded disappointed. "He was at the maximum salary my company offers for his position. He had health benefits and a retirement package. He wanted more money, had been asking for it for some time. I kept telling him no. Apparently he installed a camera in the car hoping to get some blackmail leverage over me to use to raise his salary. That's how he got the footage you described. He came to me with it, threatening to go public unless I gave the raise he demanded."

"How long ago was this?"

"About a month ago."

"And you didn't think to warn me?" Adrianna asked, getting upset.

"I didn't know he'd send it to you specifically."

"But if he was after you, why did he send the DVD to my address?"

"Sammy was a bit more than a driver to me. He was a confidant too. That's why his attempted blackmail was so disappointing. I told him things I've never told anyone else. I told him about you and that I loved you. Maybe he concluded that if he sent you the recording you'd influence me to give him what he wanted to prevent him from spreading the DVD further."

"He must have gotten my address off my suitcase tags," Adrianna mused.

"You said the envelope that the DVD came in was addressed to your husband. How did Sammy get his name?"

"I borrowed one of Christopher's cases when I came down. An old tag with his name was on it."

"I'm so sorry this happened Adrianna. Is there anything I can do to fix this? Talk to your husband maybe?"

"Oh, God! No!" Horrified at the idea, she didn't hear the teasing in his voice.

"I was joking, Adrianna, but if I could I would fix it for you. I want you to be happy, preferably with me, but if not then your husband will certainly do."

She smiled at the teasing in his tone this time. "Thanks, Trey. You're a nice guy."

"Nice." She heard the grimace in his voice. "Sexy, handsome, or you're the guy I love would work."

Adrianna kept quiet.

"No. I'll settle for nice then," he said wryly.

"Bye, Trey."

"Bye, Adrianna. I'll deal with Sammy. He won't be sending anymore DVDs. You have my word."

The promise came a little late. Her marriage was already damaged by the DVD. Nevertheless, Adrianna appreciated Trey's effort to fix things. "Thanks," she told him.

"I love you," he responded.

She rang off but didn't return the declaration. It would only be true if she said it to one man—the man who didn't want to hear it right now—her husband.

CHAPTER XIX

Christopher didn't come home until nearly the end of the following week. He'd come in the house when she wasn't there. His toothbrush and other personal care items, some of his clothing, and about three pairs of his work boots were gone. Two of his suits and a pair of dress shoes were also missing. She supposed he went to church somewhere, but certainly not First Mountain Spring where they had their membership. She hadn't seen him there on Saturday. He'd responded to the text message she'd sent about the doctor with a terse, *Are you okay?* text. Adrianna had considered replying that she was at death's door but couldn't bring herself to be dishonest. Besides, she had already told enough lies. So she just said she was okay.

***

It was Thursday, one week and two days since he'd left, that he returned. She had the tap running in the kitchen and didn't hear him come in.

"Hi, Dri."

Adrianna jerked at the sudden sound of his voice behind her and whirled to face him, her heart pumping hard. Standing there with his hair lower than the last time she'd seen him like he'd paid the Barber a recent visit, he was appealing. In loafers, blue Jeans, and a white polo shirt tucked neatly into his jeans, he looked so handsome. Adrianna wanted to rush over and embrace him in the tightest, strongest hug she could give, thankful that he'd finally come home. Looking at his stern, unsmiling face, she didn't dare.

"Hi," she returned his greeting softly.

"I need to talk to you."

If her heart wasn't already speeding to maximum capacity, it would have accelerated. He needed to talk to her not 'we' need to talk. "Now?" She asked to be sure. At his nod, she turned off the tap and went into the living room. She sat on the sofa and was disappointed but not surprised when he took one of the two armchairs in the room instead of sitting beside her. She forced a smile and asked, "What did you want to talk about?"

"Emily."

Adrianna stiffened at the sound of the child's name. "What about her?" she asked warily.

"She's mine," he announced without preamble.

Her heart slammed with disappointment. She'd been hoping that it was not the case. The 'our family' concept she had included her, Christopher, and a child both of them made, not one from another woman's body. But things were what they were. She had to accept it. "Okay. I'd like to get to know her."

He glared at her. Dri wondered what she'd done now.

"Don't lie to me Adrianna. I hate it and I hate you when you do it. It reminds me of all that's standing between us."

"I'm not ly—"

"Stop!" The word punched the air fast like a bullet and got the desired effect. Adrianna kept quiet. "You know you don't mean that. You weren't happy when you heard about her first and you aren't happy now. The delay in your response to the news that she is mine is a dead giveaway."

"Are you done chastising me and putting me in my place?" Adrianna asked, keeping her voice even, although her temper was starting to percolate at his words and attitude towards her.

"That's not what I was doing."

Maybe he hadn't intended to but things were what they were. "I would like to get to know her because she's going to be a part of this family. What support arrangements did you make with her mother and what about visitation?"

"That's not your concern."

He might as well have slapped her. Adrianna didn't think it would have hurt as much as his callous, indifferent words. She worked through the insult and responded. "Actually it is. Our finances are joined and what affects you affects me and this family."

"You keep saying family," her husband burst out in frustration, struggling to contain anger, the battle etched in the hard set of his jaw and the temper flaring in his eyes. "What family are you referring to? You keep talking in the first person plural, using 'we', 'us' and 'our'. There's none of that where we are concerned. You made sure of that when you slept with another man."

"I did not sleep with him, Chris."

"Adrianna, I didn't come home to talk about your unfaithfulness. I just want you to know that Emily is mine and I intend to support her."

She couldn't deny totally the classification of her being unfaithful. By letting another man kiss and touch her the way Trey had, she had violated the sacredness of her marriage. Thinking it wise not to say anything more on that subject for now, she talked about his daughter. "How do you intend to support her? Will she visit or will you go and visit? What's the financial support going to be?"

"I'll go visit her for now. I don't want to bring her into this." He waved his hand around.

Into this? What did he mean? Was he talking about the chasm between them? She asked him. "What don't you want to bring her into?"

"Dri, kids are sensitive and with the differences between us now, I wouldn't want her picking up the strain. Besides, I'm not going to bring her where she's not wanted."

"I didn't say I didn't want her here," she snapped, irritated.

"You implied it by all your talk about the cost to this family."

"I was stating facts and looking at the situation practically, Christopher. I have nothing against your daughter. I—"

"You have nothing against *my* daughter." He gave her a cool look. "That's what I'm talking about. You can't even use her name. If you can't bear to speak it, how are you going to make her feel welcome here?"

Adrianna studied his face. The hostility in his gaze and the unyielding set of his mouth told her that she couldn't win. He would twist everything she said like he just did and had been doing, no matter how innocent her statement or the intent behind it. Christopher despised her. The dislike on his countenance was unmistakable. Nothing she said or did would please him. What she did with Trey, she surmised, was in the forefront of his mind. He couldn't shake the images he'd seen, and every time he looked at her, she reminded him of her indiscretion with another man. He'd come home to tell her about Emily, he'd said, but they needed to talk about the DVD. She took initiative, even though she strongly suspected he'd try to shut her down.

"It was an aberration in judgment," she said calmly, maintaining eye contact despite the disdain in his eyes.

He got what she was referring to immediately. "An aberration!" he snapped. "An aberration is ten seconds of bad judgment. This was almost five minutes!"

"Christopher, I swear I've never cheated on you."

"What do you call what you did with that man?"

"I meant I never slept with him." At least not while I've been married to you, she added in her head.

"And do you think that lessens the evil of what you did?" he asked contemptuously.

Adrianna didn't think it wise to answer that. Instead she said, "Chris, I'm sorry for what I did. There's no excuse for it and no explanation."

"Adrianna, for a man to handle you the way he did, you had to have known him before. The question in my mind is, how long have you been carrying on with him?"

Adrianna took a breath and then took the plunge she'd been hoping to avoid—giving the background on Trey. "Ten years ago, and *long* before I met you," she emphasized, "I knew him."

She studied her fingernails, feeling embarrassed about what she was about to admit. "I was in church then, but not serious about God. I dated Trey and w-we were..." she trailed off not wanting to publicly admit that she'd been a fornicator and to her husband at that. Christopher didn't help her. When she chanced a glance at him, she couldn't tell how he was reacting to her words. His expression was wooden. "We were intimate," she mumbled.

"So the trip to Jamaica was a reunion of sorts?" he asked his tone icy and full of sarcasm.

"*No it was not.*" Adrianna gave every word precise stress to be very clear. "I went to talk about meeting the design needs for his company. I didn't know at the time that the business was his."

"You usually research a company. How come you didn't know?" he asked suspiciously.

"He had some of the information on the website changed to reflect a different name and had his picture taken down."

"Are you really trying to say that he lured you there?" He asked in a *do-you-take-me-for-a-fool* way.

"Chris, if I had known he was the one, I wouldn't have gone down there."

"Why? Because you still wanted him and knew you'd end up sleeping with him?" The question was harsh and his expression full of repugnance.

"I never planned to do that." Adrianna realized that what she said sounded like an admission of adultery. She opened her mouth to clarify her statement, but he got his words in before hers.

"It just happened out of the blue then—an aberration in judgment like you said."

"It didn't happen at all," she insisted.

"Right," he said sarcastically.

Adrianna shifted to the right end of the sofa to be near him and reached for his left hand resting on his knee. Before he could snatch it away, she trapped his hand in both of hers and held on tighter as he tried to pull away. "Christopher," she started, meeting his antagonistic gaze, "I swear I did not sleep with him. The trip to Jamaica was for business, not some pre-planned rendezvous with him. I haven't been in touch with him since we broke up ten years ago. The Jamaica trip was the first time that I met him after so many years."

He watched her for a long time without saying a word, his expression still aggressive but with the barest hint of uncertainty in it, or maybe that was what she was hoping for. "If you haven't seen him or been in touch with him, why did you allow him the liberties that you did?"

Adrianna compressed her lips and her gaze fell before the intensity of his. "It was a mistake that I regret from the depth of my soul."

"That didn't answer my question. Why did you let him kiss you? Why did you allow him to touch you?"

She couldn't say because the answer that she had would only make a bad situation worse.

"Why!"

Adrianna jumped at his sudden shout and lost her grip on his hand. She propped shaking elbows on quivering knees and pressed her fingertips to her eyelids as she felt the familiar sting of tears. "B-because I-I was l-lonely," she stuttered. "Because I felt empty and needed comfort."

"I was the one who should have filled you, Dri," he gritted. "*I*" he emphasized and she peeked through her fingers to see him jab his chest, "was the one, *the only one*, with the right to comfort you. Yet before you left for Jamaica you wouldn't let me. But you willingly accepted the embrace, kisses, and touches of a man who was a former lover. Where does that leave me, Dri? What does that leave me to believe about you?"

"Chris, it was one time, one mistake, one case of bad judgment. I've never done it before and will never do it again. I'm asking, begging for your forgiveness."

"I know that I have to forgive you Adrianna. It's the Christian thing to do. The problem is that I don't trust you now and don't know if I ever will. You deceived me before when you got pregnant without telling me and I feel like you've done the same thing again. You slept with this man once. The fact that you went into his arms willingly after all this time suggests to me that you still have feelings for him."

"No I—"

"Let me finish!"

Adrianna clasped her hands in her lap and kept silent.

"You'd never have let him kiss and touch you if you didn't want his attention. What's irking me and making me disgusted is that after you left his arms, you brought your tainted body to me and slept with me the night you came home."

The revulsion in his tone was so thick, Adrianna felt the weight of it even heavier than the sin she'd committed.

"If that's not deception I don't know what is. The only conclusion I can draw as to your reason for doing that is your fear that you might be pregnant, which it turns out that you are. I'm not claiming that child until you do a DNA test."

Adrianna's temper had started percolating from the time he called her 'tainted'. His accusing her of sleeping with Trey once too many times now made her mad. The last straw was the reason he claimed that he thought she did it; and to add insult to injury, he wanted a DNA test before he claimed his child. You know what? Forget this. She'd done wrong. That was true. She had apologized over and over and over again. What did he want her to do? Beg, grovel, or prostrate herself on the ground? She felt like she'd already done that from the number of his insults she had tolerated, and his abuse. The marks on her neck were fading, but they were still visible. She wore a scarf like she had been doing all week. Adrianna stood and looked down at him, anger making her eyes flash. "Listen, I've done you wrong. I know that. I'm a slut. I get it. I prostituted myself with a man, you said. I took that too, knowing you had a right to be angry, understanding that anger fueled that kind of talk. I figured if it got rid of your rage to call me a whore I could take it."

Adrianna stopped, the pain of repeating his opinion of her catching her off guard. It hurt to hear her husband call her those things and think those things about her. She swallowed and tried to press on. The anger that had pushed her to her feet suddenly deserted her, leaving her feeling emotionally weak, hollow, and very vulnerable. "On the night I came home from Jamaica I walked into your arms because I wanted to do it, not because I had to do it to cover up a pregnancy. The lack of feeling I told you I was experiencing had gone away. After our conversation, the one we had when I was down there, I came to the realization that I didn't want our marriage to end and that my keeping you at a distance was going to cause divorce. I didn't want that. It was kind of like how you woke up and realized you needed to stop treating me badly when I had the miscarriage. I needed to fully forgive you and let go the memories of your mistreatment. I couldn't wait to get home after that. You said I gave you my tainted body but I never had sex with him, which is what I think you meant. If you feel that I'm tainted because he touched and kissed me, then I guess I'll always be dirty to you because I can't reverse the wrong that I did. I can't reverse that mistake. I wish to God that I could but I can't."

Adrianna searched his face, looking for some sort of relenting in his countenance, some sign that she was getting through to him, but she didn't find anything. Instead, his expression grew increasingly closed with every word she spoke. Desperation pushed her to her knees before her husband. She grasped both his hands in hers and was grateful that he didn't pull away. "Chris, I'm sorry, really, truly sorry. I'm pleading for your forgiveness. You did me wrong and I forgave you. Now I'm the one who is wrong and in need of your forgiveness. Please don't withhold it from me. I've been worried all week, wondering where you were. The only reason I didn't lose it was because Douglas said you were okay and he knew where you were. He wouldn't tell even though I asked. I didn't know if you would come back, I didn't know what you would do, and I still don't know. All I'm asking for is a chance to show you that I'm worth your love." Now the shoe was on the other foot, she understood how her husband had felt when he asked her the same thing after her miscarriage and when she kept him at a distance. "I love you, Christopher. I *love* you." She leaned in to kiss him and felt the rejection like a blade slashing her heart asunder when he pulled back sharply with a look of distaste. Her entire body burned with shame at his rebuff. Releasing his hands in case he snubbed her even more and dragged them from her grasp, she pushed to her feet and whispered, "I'm sorry," both for trying to kiss him and for the wrong she had done. Holding herself stiff and erect so she wouldn't physically collapse, she climbed the stairs to her room and closed the door quietly behind her before breaking down.

From his position in the living room, Christopher listened to the muffled sounds of his wife's sobs. A part of him yearned to climb the stairs and comfort her, but another part of him kept seeing her in another man's arms and he didn't move. His brother-in-law had said he might never understand why Dri did what she did but they had to come to the place where they moved on from this. Christopher admitted to himself that he wasn't at that place yet and wasn't sure he would ever get there.

CHAPTER XX

Seven months later

Christopher pulled his truck into the side yard of the house Vivene was renting in the town of Heart Haven. It was the second week in June and she'd moved in two weeks ago. Wanting Emily to be closer to her father, she had waited until the school year finished before making the journey across the country. She was a nurse and had gotten a position with the local Heart Haven Hospital. She also worked on a per diem basis with some other hospitals and she'd been called in to work today, her day off from Heart Haven Hospital. Having no babysitting back up for Emily she'd called him. He agreed to watch Emily while Vivene worked the 3-11 pm shift. He'd asked a lady from church to cover for him from three to seven since that's the time he could make it.

Christopher stepped out of his truck into the sweltering early June sunshine that he'd worked and sweated in all day. He followed the brick path from the side yard to the front of the building. He stepped up on the porch and rang the bell. While he waited, he admired what Vivene had done with the decking. It had been a dull blue before. With the landlord's permission, she'd had it painted a richer hue of blue. Turquoise, she said, but he still called it blue, a color that matched the railing supported by white balusters. There were potted plants fringing the base of the railing and on either side of the front door, and against the white siding on the house. She had all types of plants out here: Hyacinth, orchids, tulips, dahlias, carnations, lilies and lots of foliage. In the six months since he'd discovered that Emily was his child, he'd found out a bit about Vivene and one thing they shared in common was a love of plants. He smiled a little as he thought that their conversations surrounded Emily and flowers.

"It's my daddy, Mrs. Dover," he heard Emily declare from the other side of the door.

"I know that dear, but you never open the door until you make sure," the elderly lady's reply came out mildly chiding.

Christopher grinned as he thought that the woman must be glad her relief had come. Emily was a chatter box and could wear down your ears and your resolve when she wanted something badly.

As soon as Mrs. Dover opened the door, Emily rushed out and embraced him. Christopher's heart shifted with tenderness at her warmth and love. Her hugs were the only ones he got these days, and they went a long way to soothing his lonely heart. Things at home were strained most days and outright tense on others. Adrianna was almost a month away from delivery. As he'd watched her stomach grow over these past months, his disquiet about the issue of paternity had intensified. Had his wife spoken the truth that the baby was his? Christopher wanted to believe her claim, but there was a small pocket of doubt that wouldn't let go. She was due soon, and Christopher wondered sometimes if the doctor was mistaken and there really was more than one child in there. He never realized a woman's belly could stretch that much. The weight was heavy he knew because he often noticed her massaging her back and wanted more than once to do it for her but always held back. Since his rejection of her kiss that afternoon last November, she'd gone out of her way not to touch him. If they met each other on the stairs, she'd either go back to the top if he was coming up or the reverse if he was coming down. She moved out of his path in such an obvious way that it had started to irritate him.

"Daddy, aren't you glad to see me?" Emily demanded, snatching him from his thoughts.

"Sure I am, Sugar." He smiled down at her and lifted her high as she reached up to him.

"Why were you frowning then?"

Christopher hadn't been aware of that. More than likely his thoughts had caused it. "I'm smiling now," he said tickling her. She giggled and squirmed.

"Can you take me to the park? Mrs. Dover didn't want to go." She cupped her hand at his ear and whispered the last part.

"Okay, Em, but let me at least get something to drink first and take a five minute rest. Then I'll take you."

"Deal," She said, squirming to get down now that she'd gotten her heart's desire, a hug from her daddy and a trip to the park. She skipped back inside, calling over her shoulder, "I made lemonade."

If it was anything like the one she'd given him last week, it would need lots of water. Otherwise he would develop diabetes overnight. Mrs. Dover reappeared with her purse as he was about to close the door.

"I'll be on my way now, Bro. Reid," She said.

"One minute," Christopher delayed her. He fished his wallet from his rear pocket, counted out some bills and placed them in her hand.

"Oh, that's too much," she protested.

He folded her fingers over the cash as she tried to return one of the twenties. Mrs. Dover was a widow without family. All she had coming in was social security. She came every time he called her and she was good with Emily. Despite her age, she was patient and kind with the energetic little girl. Christopher appreciated her. "It's not," he contradicted gently, shaking his head and smiling. "Besides, the extra's for when I call you emergency next time."

"Oh you." She fluttered her hand at him but with a pleased smile. "Thank you, Bro. Reid," she said, her voice filled with appreciation.

He watched her walk down the steps to the gate where her 1980 Toyota Camry was parked and waited until she got in and drove away before closing the front door.

He turned around to find Emily with a glass of juice in one hand and her flip flops in the other. "Here, Daddy, drink this, and then we can go," she offered, extending the glass of lemonade to him, at least he hoped it was lemonade. It was pink rather than its usual color. Christopher accepted it and took a hesitant sip. Umm. Not bad. He downed the contents of the glass.

"Great!" Emily exclaimed, grabbing the empty glass from him and resting it on the bottom step of the stairs leading to the second level of the house. Vivene was renting the lower level only. The landlord lived upstairs but used a different entrance. "Can we go now?" She asked, dancing with eagerness.

"What about my rest?" Christopher protested as she unlocked the front door.

"You can rest while you drive to the park," she said, hurrying outside, her twists bouncing around her cute head.

Christopher smiled and shook his head, following her and closing the door behind him. No rest for the weary, it seemed. At forty two, he was getting kind of old to keep up with a kid Emily's age and after a day of physical labor too. To add to that he'd have a baby in his house soon. Some of those tiny people took a long time to sleep through the night, he'd heard. Anyway, it was too late to back out now, he thought, as he held the passenger door of his truck open while Emily scrambled inside. He was already in the marriage. The only way was forward. As he prayed and fired up the engine, it didn't even cross his mind that the baby he just thought about might not even be his.

CHAPTER XXI

Adrianna turned every way she could to get comfortable but failed. She didn't have a lot of sleeping options. On her back was one of the few ways she could get to sleep these days, but the ache that had been present all day in her lower back had escalated as the night wore on. Great! Now she wanted to pee. She had to get up. She rolled to her left side and inched up on her elbow until she was upright. As she scooted slowly forward, her sphincter muscle battled to contain pee under the weight of her belly. Hurry, hurry, she told herself, which was easier said than done these days with the mini football field in front of her. Not bothering with her house slippers, she waddled into the bathroom and made it just in time.

Done with her business, Adrianna lathered and rinsed her hands. She reached for the hand towel to dry and felt a sudden and warm rush of liquid between her thighs. Frozen, her hands in mid-air and afraid to look down, she stood there. The last time this had happened she had lost her baby. Frightened, terrified that when she looked down she might find a color she had come to dread, all she saw was a pool of clear liquid on the floor of the bathroom and her legs felt wet. Her water had broken. She heaved a huge sigh. No sign of blood was good. And then as the implication of her water breaking registered, she panicked. She was having the baby! Tonight! Right now possibly. How much was she dilated? Where were the promised labor pains—not that she was looking forward to those. But was something wrong since they hadn't come? Over the past two weeks, she'd been having low voltage period pains as she described them to Dr. Island. They were Braxton Hicks, the doctor had said. The real labor pain would be much more severe and occur more frequently. Today no Braxton's had hit. What gives then? It was time to call Dr. Island.

Adrianna was half way into her room when the first pain hit. She had to stop and pant like an overheated dog. The doctor had been right. There was a distinct difference between Braxton Hicks and the real thing. Taking it slow and easy, she straightened and made it to the phone. The doctor listened to everything Adrianna told her and said that when the contractions were five minutes apart she needed to go to the hospital. As soon as she hung up the phone, Dri sank to her knees. Bracing her hands on her thighs, she tried to breathe like they told her in Lamaze class but it didn't help, and she panted like they told her not to until she nearly hyperventilated. By the time the contraction passed, she felt so weak that it took her a while to get off the floor. Forcing her brain to work, she looked at her watch and calculated that about six minutes had passed between her water breaking and the end of her conversation with the doctor. It was time to go to the hospital. Her bag was packed, but she couldn't go to the hospital wet and icky like this. She had to wash up and put on some street clothes.

In the tub another contraction sent her to her knees again. By the time she found an undergarment and a maternity summer dress, she barely survived two more. Her maternity bag. Where was it? Armoire. Right. She got the bag and headed for the door as fast as she could, praying that she could drive and that she would get to the car before any more contractions. No such luck. She made it to the head of the stairs and cried out in agony.

**

Christopher raised his head from his pillow. He'd gotten in after midnight, taken a shower and laid his head down. He was drifting off when he heard somebody cry out. After that he heard what sounded like hoo, hoo, hee, hee. What? He threw off the sheet and got out of bed at the sound of a lengthy, pain-filled moan. He opened his room door to see Adrianna seated at the top of the stairs with a bag next to her.

"Dri?"

No answer. Only more *hoo, hoo, hee, hee.*

She gripped the banister and got up slowly, her entire body

shaking. Christopher rushed to her, fearful that she would fall down the stairs. He saw the tears and pain on her face, and from the way she held her belly, his sleepy brain realized she was in labor. Why hadn't she called him? "Sit down," he commanded, easing her back down. "I'll throw on something quick and take you to the hospital."

She sat. He figured she must be in a great deal of pain because she hadn't taken any help from him in the past six months, not even when it was a struggle to carry something on her own. When he came back out in Jeans and with his shirt unbuttoned, she was easing down the stairs, step by step on her bottom. He grabbed the bag and got to the bottom before she did. She stood at the final step and started moving to the front door with her hand braced against the wall. At the door she stopped again and gripped the handle so hard that Christopher thought her knuckles would break through her skin. She breathed in short, fast gasps.

Christopher stood there feeling helpless, wanting to relieve her pain and feeling impotent that he could do nothing to ease her agony. "Let me carry you to the truck," he offered because he didn't know what else to say when her breathing evened out and she opened the front door.

She shook her head. "No," she said quickly as if oxygen was in short supply. "You might drop me. I can't lose a third baby."

Christopher watched his wife's retreating back stunned. Third baby? He thought this was her second. Hurrying after her when she doubled over in pain half way to the truck, he told himself that this was not the time for questions.

***

Aisha Karen Reid was born four hours later. She was pink, wrinkled and long with a full head of bushy and soft curls. Although exhausted and sleepy in the extreme, Adrianna noticed the glowing smile that spread across her husband's face and the gentle way he cradled his daughter in his big hands. He held her next to his heart and Adrianna hoped their baby had truly found a place there. Did he accept this little girl as his own or would he want undeniable proof? She was willing to provide it, but in her heart it would mean so much if he were to accept their baby without the DNA testing. To Dri it would mean that her faithfulness was no longer a matter of trust between them. She drifted off, feeling a little envious of Aisha that she had the luxury of being held by Christopher when she, Dri, longed so much for it but knew he would never hold tainted goods again.

***

That afternoon

Karen, Douglas, and their kids had come to see Adrianna. Esther was excited that her cousin was a girl. She had two brothers, now, Jonah and Jared, who was born last December, and she desperately wanted a sister. Since Karen wasn't having anymore children, Esther said that Aisha would be her cousin and her sister. They spent about forty minutes visiting and left shortly before Christopher came back.

Adrianna looked up from breastfeeding Aisha towards the soft knock at the hospital room's door. Her heart leapt at the sight of the clean shaven and attractive man standing at the door: Her husband. He'd changed into a white open collar, cotton shirt and blue jeans with seams pressed to razor sharp perfection. He said his pants should be able to stand on their own, and they could only do that with perfect seams. His sleeves were rolled three quarters of the way up, exposing the strength of his arms and the Michael Kors watch she'd bought for him two Christmases ago.

"I got you something," he said, stopping by her bedside and removing his sunglasses. He brought his hand from behind his back to reveal a white fuzzy mother bear cradling a cub in her arms. A red heart with the words 'I Love You' was attached to mother and child.

"Ohhhh," she said softly, taking it and brushing its soft fur against her cheek. She loved stuffed animals. He used to surprise her with them. She hadn't gotten one in a while. The fact that he thought to bring this sent warm and gentle feelings through her heart. "Thank you." She looked up with a smile full of more appreciation for him than she intended to show.

Christopher met his wife's gaze and couldn't find air. He reached for a tie that wasn't there—his throat felt that constricted. Over the last seven months, each of them had pretty much kept out of the others way, keeping their communication to matters mostly related to the house. He always asked about how she was feeling. She always replied okay and moved on. He offered to make the doctor's visits with her, but she never told him when she was going. After a while he didn't ask about it. He too came and went at will and didn't keep her informed of his whereabouts. He figured she would call him if she needed him. Last night though, he realized how determined she was not to need him when he found her trying to make it to the hospital on her own. Over time he had begun to wonder if the love she had professed after he discovered her indiscretion with Trey had been just words. Right now though, the message she seemed to be conveying was that those three words were still true. Douglas had said a time would come where both of them would let go the past even if they didn't understand all the mess that had happened. Christopher felt like he had reached that place. There was something he needed to do, to tell his wife so that she would know what he was thinking. He cleared his throat.

"How's she doing?" he asked, running his fingers lightly over Aisha's springy, black curls.

"Fine. She's eating and sleeping and soiling diapers like she's supposed to," Adrianna laughed.

He smiled a little and cleared his throat again. Adrianna looked at him with a slight frown. "Are you okay? You're not getting sick, are you?" She sounded worried.

"Don't worry. I won't infect her with anything."

"That didn't cross my mind. I was concerned about you."

"You were?" His brows arched upwards in surprise.

She looked away and cleared her throat.

"Something contagious, isn't it?" he grinned, referring to the throat-clearing.

"And it's called awkwardness," she muttered, easing Aisha off her breast.

Christopher swallowed as he got an eyeful of her exposed chest. Awkwardness wasn't the only thing he was feeling now. A healthy dose of arousal had joined it too. He pulled up a chair and sat down quickly in case Adrianna saw the evidence of it. She covered herself, and Christopher sighed in relief and nearly groaned in agony as she opened the other side of her nightgown and switched the baby to the other breast.

"Chris?"

His wife's question jerked his eyes open. Christopher wasn't aware that he'd closed them against the temptation of her body. If he kept looking below her chin he would brush his daughter aside and put his head where Aisha's had been. Without meaning to he cleared his throat.

"Maybe you need some cough drops," Adrianna suggested with an innocent expression, but the sparkle in her eyes belied her teasing.

"Maybe," he murmured. What he needed was her, but that wasn't possible right now. And then there was the problem between them—the paternity issue. "Dri, I wanted to talk to you about the paternity mat—

"We can do the DNA test today," she cut in, suddenly looking everywhere but at him. "As a matter of fact, the phle—"

A knock on the door had them both looking towards the entrance of the room. A middle aged Caucasian woman stood there with some papers in her hands. "Hi," she said, "I'm Genna, the phlebotomist. I understand I'm to take some samples for DNA testing." She walked over to them, not noticing the strained silence in the room. "Who are the patients?" she asked with a smile.

"All of us," Adrianna answered, easing a now sleeping Aisha off her breast and covering herself. She put the baby to her shoulder and burped her.

"Can you give us a minute?" Christopher asked the phlebotomist.

Both women, his wife and the phlebotomist, turned to him with inquiring looks.

"Sure," Genna agreed, picking up the paperwork from the foot of Adrianna's bed. "I'll be back in a half hour. Enough time?" She directed her question at Christopher.

"An hour."

"You got it. See you at four." She left, closing the door behind her.

"Dri, I don't want to do the testing," Christopher said as the door clicked.

"Why not? Don't you want to be sure Aisha's yours?" Adrianna continued patting her baby's back, hoping that her pounding heart would not awaken the child. Why didn't he want the testing done? Did he believe her? If yes, what did that mean?

"I believe you."

Adrianna caught her sigh of relief, not certain after so long where they went from here. What brought him to this conclusion when seven months ago he thought she was lying? What had changed his mind? Opening her eyes and moistening her lips, she said, "I thought you believed I was a liar and a cheat."

"Not anymore. I love you."

Three precious words spoken so easily by him; three words that she would have given up anything to have heard seven months ago when she got on her knees before him, begged for his forgiveness, and told him she loved him. Dare she believe them now? "I thought you said I was tainted," she murmured low, feeling a little shaky and a lot weepy as she remembered the disdain with which he had treated her.

"Here, let me take her," Christopher offered to take Aisha instead of responding to what she said. Dri relinquished her because the shakes were turning to tremors and she didn't want to wake her up. She watched him walk around the bed and lay their daughter in the incubator by her bedside. When he circled back around the bed again, he didn't sit in the chair. Instead, he perched on the edge of the bed and shifted sideways. His thigh pressed against her hip and Adrianna jerked. He got off the bed at once. "Did I hurt you?" he asked tensely.

Adrianna shook her head and willed herself to be calm. His nearness made her nervous. She wanted to lean into him and feel his warmth and his strength but wasn't sure that he would welcome her. The effort to keep her craving for his touch to herself made her uncomfortable. So starved for his attention, a little contact with him was like a sharp jolt of pleasurable electricity. "Sit down," she said, patting the sheet beside her. He wanted to talk and she was open to it. He said that he loved her and she wanted to hear it again. Forcing her craving for his attention aside and suppressing her reaction to contact with him, she said, "You didn't hurt me, Chris."

He sat down gingerly this time, but didn't touch her. He braced his hand on the bed, palm down, and Dri nearly reached out to touch him. She made a fist so she wouldn't yield to the pull. Adrianna repeated the statement he hadn't responded to. Tracing her fingers over the rough hospital sheet covering her lap she said, "I thought you believed I was tainted."

The weight of the sigh that emerged from his lips sounded like it had travelled a long and winding road to his mouth. "Adrianna, I said a lot of things to you last year in anger. At the time I was torn up inside and I wanted you to bleed, or rather hemorrhage as much as I was hemorrhaging."

"And now?" She held her breath.

"Now, I don't care about any of that. I admit that it's been a real struggle to get past the picture of you in another man's arms. I've been praying and asking God to remove my bitterness and disillusionment with what happened. He's come through for me, Dri." He smiled and she returned it. "When I look at you now I don't feel the anger I used to feel. I only experience a desire to repair the rift between us. I only feel the need to be free with my wife—free to talk and laugh and play. I want our friendship back, Dri. I want our marriage back." He reached out and took her hand. Adrianna gripped his fingers like he'd offered a lifeline, and indeed he had. It was a lifeline of love and an offer to save their marriage. "I've reached the point where what you did matters less than what we have or can have, which is a loving marriage full of loyalty, commitment and trust. The Bible tells us that faith is the substance of what we hope for and the evidence of what we don't see. I believe our marriage can be fixed Adrianna and that it will be stronger than what we had before. I have faith in this. I know I love you. My heart is full of tenderness towards you. The way you looked at me earlier with the same tenderness that I feel in my heart gives me hope that you also believe that we have something worth fighting for. With willing hearts and trust in God, I believe we can make it and our marriage can survive. Do you believe this Adrianna?"

"I do," she whispered.

He let out a long, fast breath as if he'd been holding quite a bit of air in check while building up to her answer. He raised her hand to his lips and kissed it. "If we believe together and trust in God, I think—I know we will make it. Months ago you asked me to forgive you and I never answered. I'm answering now. I forgive you, Adrianna. Will you forgive me for all these months of neglecting you and being mad at you?"

Her heart sang at her husband's words and joy spread at his forgiveness. Fighting tears, Adrianna murmured, "There's nothing to forgive. I'm the one who did wrong. I'm the one in need of pardon. I hurt you, robbed you, but as God is my witness, Chris, I will never hurt you again."

He squeezed her hand gently and kissed it again to show his acceptance. "I need to ask you something, Dri."

"What?" She looked at him quizzically.

"What do you see when you look at me? Do you only see a man

who almost choked you to death or do you see a man whom you could learn to love again?"

Adrianna didn't know why Christopher was asking her these questions, but she was sensitive enough to know that with all that had transpired, her husband would not know that she still loved him unless she said it.

"How do you view me, Dri?" he asked again, looking uneasy that she didn't answer right away.

Adrianna tugged on his hand for him to move closer. He did. "I see," she began, smiling and letting her affection for him show in the gentle curve of her lips, the warmth and love in her eyes, and in the soft caress of her fingers over his. "I see a man who loves me even though I don't deserve it. I see a wonderful man with a big, open, and forgiving heart. I'm eternally grateful to God for that man. I praise God for you and I thank you, Chris, for giving me, us, a second chance. I love you."

He raised her hand to his lips again but turned it over. He touched his lips to her fingertips and charted a trail of soft, sweet kisses across her palm to her wrist, stopping half way to tickle and tantalize the tender, sensitive skin with his tongue.

Adrianna's breath whistled at the intimacy of his touch and her heart fluttered with feelings that she had held in check for too long because she didn't know if she were loved. When he pressed her hand against his heart and she felt the accelerated pounding of that organ, a thrill coursed through her that their closeness had affected him too.

"I need to know something else Adrianna. I see you every day, trying to avoid me in the house, trying to make yourself inconspicuous when we're in the same room together."

"You noticed?" she asked softly.

"I have and it bothers me when you do that. Why do you hurry out of my way like you think I'm going to hurt you?"

Adrianna bit her lip and stared at her sheet draped toes at the foot of the bed. "You said you hated me, and every time you looked at me, your face became so angry and disgusted that I've been trying to keep out of your way. I thought that if you didn't see me, you'd have a chance to calm down. And then maybe, just maybe, when you were calm, you would remember that you loved me and we were married for better or worse."

"And that's the only reason?"

"Well," she said slowly, "you didn't want my touch. You made that plain last year when I tried to kiss you. So I try not to touch you when we pass by each other at home."

"Nothing more?"

Adrianna shook her head. There was one more thing, but she wouldn't tell him. It had been done in anger and he wouldn't have done it if her action hadn't driven him to lose his temper.

"What about the bruises I left right here?" He trailed a thumb and forefinger on either side of her throat.

Adrianna shivered and lifted her eyes to meet his gaze. How did he know about those?

"Karen spoke to me about it."

Dri's eyebrows knitted. She'd worn a scarf around her neck the whole time. How had her sister found out?

"She showed me pictures. She took them the night we fought and she brought you to her house. She took them while you were sleeping."

She glanced away. What could she say? The damage had already been done.

"I'm sorry, Adrianna. I never meant to hurt you."

She heard the remorse in his voice. When she met his gaze, his eyes were full of regret. "It's all right," she said. "I know you didn't mean to."

He slid his palm to the base of her neck and cupped his hand there. "Are you afraid when I touch you Dri?" he asked, sounding sad.

"Only that you'll stop," she whispered.

He shifted so more of his body was on the bed. The warmth from his thigh seeped through the sheet to hers as he pressed against her. "Would you mind if I kissed you Dri?"

"I would mind if you didn't," she said, watching his mouth approach with hungry impatience. The kiss was unhurried, deep, and delicious. It carried seven months of apology, a lifetime of love, and promise of a better future. When they let air filter between them, the unspoken words of the kiss became audible; and they lost count of the number of times they declared their love for each other.

A long time later, Christopher toed off his shoes and lay beside his wife, exchanging touches and kisses. A knock on the door interrupted their intimacy. Genna popped her head in. "I'm back," she said with a smile, which got bigger when she saw them together. "I'm getting the feeling you don't need DNA testing anymore."

"No, we don't," Christopher said confidently.

With a grin and wave, she left.

"Chris, you could still get it done," Dri suggested, knowing she was saying it for his peace of mind rather than hers.

"Why?" he asked, looking like he didn't understand why she'd even suggested it. "I love you, Adrianna, and I trust you. I asked God to fix our marriage and trust Him to do it. I think He began the restoration today. I believe God wants us to be together, Dri. Otherwise we wouldn't be in agreement right now. I believe He has given me back my wife. You are my gift from Him and because He only gives what is good I trust you. I believe you when you say nothing happened. That mean's Aisha is mine." He propped himself up on an elbow when Adrianna started weeping. "Oh, boy, what did I say now? Why are you crying?" He fished his already wet handkerchief from his pocket and dried her eyes. He'd mopped up twice already.

"You trust me?" she sniffed.

"I thought I just said that."

"Oh, Chris, it means everything to me to hear you say that. I love you," she confessed and kissed him until his head spun.

When his world stopped turning, Christopher placed a hand on his wife's abdomen and said, "Forgive this question Dri, but I ache for you. How long before we can...you know?" he asked, his hand moving lightly over her abdomen.

Adrianna giggled. "Six to eight weeks according to the doctor."

He sighed. "Oh, well. I've waited seven months. What's two more?"

She laughed and then got serious. "I don't want any secrets between us ever again."

Christopher nodded, thinking it was a good idea.

"So I need to tell you something—two things actually."

He tensed, wondering what was about to break over their heads and ruin their new found peace and love.

"I think in all my pain earlier my tongue slipped and I confessed that I had two miscarriages rather than one."

"You did," he said quietly, glad she had brought it up. It was something he had planned to discuss in the future. "After Trey and I separated, I found out I was pregnant. He didn't know. I didn't tell him because he was married which was why I broke off with him. I didn't know that he was at first. I lost the baby when I was nearly two months pregnant. The doctor said stress caused it."

When he didn't speak, Adrianna asked, "What are you thinking?"

He smiled and tweaked her nose. "I'm glad you told me, but it doesn't matter because it doesn't affect our lives, our love, or our future.

She smiled big. "I love you, Christopher Reid."

"Keep it coming. I won't get tired of hearing it." He grinned. "What's the second thing you need to tell me?"

"It was Trey's former employee who sent that DVD. The guy was trying to blackmail him. When Trey didn't give him the money he demanded, he sent the DVD, hoping to cause embarrassment and make Trey pay the money. He's since taken care of the guy. We won't have any more trouble with him."

"You called Trey?"

The question was mild, but Adrianna sensed that what she'd said didn't set well with Christopher. "I only called to find out if he sent the DVD to break us up. I deleted his number from my phone since then." Dri searched Christopher's expression uncertainly, worried he didn't believe her.

He watched her for a while and then grinned. "Good," he said. "I'm glad you erased his number."

Adrianna smiled in relief.

"I have one final thing I need to tell you," she said.

He watched her warily. "Another secret?"

"No." Adrianna laughed at his uneasy expression. "I need a favor."

"What's that?" he asked, running his fingers through her hair.

"Will you bring Emily to see me?"

His hand stilled and he searched her face. Adrianna smiled at him and nodded to let him know she meant it. "Seriously?" It came out as a question but the sound of it echoed with the joy of knowing the answer was affirmative.

"Seriously," she said.

This time he kissed her, pressing her into the pillows and

caressing every part of her body he could touch. When the nurse came in, she slipped right back out undetected with a huge smile, thinking that this couple would be back in the Maternity Unit within the year.

THE END

UPCOMING TITLES

Emeralds Aren't Forever
(The Banning Island Romances: Book 3)
<u>Coming Fall 2014</u>

On a Spanish American Cruise vacation, Sarah has no idea how valuable the stone on her purse's clasp is. When she nearly gets mugged in Cartagena and almost thrown overboard later, she solicits help from the man who saved her both times—Everton Marsh. An ex-revolutionary and a sometimes security specialist, Everton had wanted a peaceful vacation. This American woman, Sarah, wasn't letting that happen. Together, they uncover a ring of emerald thieves, stretching from Cartagena to New York and to all parts of the Caribbean. Danger rises for Sarah as these thieves are willing to murder whoever blocks them from the emeralds. Now more than ever she needs Everton's protection. After one slow dance on a dark deck one night, Sarah realizes that she wants more than his protection.

EXISTING TITLE

From Passion to Pleasure
(Five Brothers: Book 1)
<u>Excerpt</u>

"No, I'm not going," she objected emphatically.

"Excuse me?" He sounded like he didn't think his hearing was reliable.

"I'm not going to the caterer with you tomorrow to change the menu," she told him clearly.

"And I don't appreciate your high-handedness in dictating to me that I have to go."

"My high-handedness?" He sounded incredulous. "I never dictated anything. I clearly and deliberately used the word *suggest*."

At the moment Lauren couldn't remember what word he'd used and being in no mood to exercise her brain in recollection, she didn't even try. She was too upset and too tired and too emotional and undoubtedly tomorrow she would regret all. However, right now she wanted this man to get it into his head that he couldn't boss her around, and her opinions and feelings counted, and she would make them heard! She proceeded to do just that. "James, I told you I have a very strong objection to serving meat at the wedding, and I feel that you should consider my concerns and respect them. Frankly I feel like you're trying to railroad me into doing what I don't want to do."

"So this is all about you, is it?" The question was heated, like his control on his temper was slipping. "I don't have any input. My wishes are irrelevant. I thought for a marriage to happen two people,

120

male and female, had to be involved. Obviously you've redefined marriage to a solitary state. In short, you've cut me out of the picture. Maybe I should take you seriously and stay out of the picture."

Fear and fury clutched simultaneously at Lauren's throat and chest, restricting her air supply and making her heart thunder like train wheels clattering over railroad tracks. Was he trying to break their engagement? The question floated fleetingly as fury rose higher; and like a Tsunami roaring in from the depths of the ocean to the shore, it exploded into a raging torrent of words that Lauren would later wish she hadn't said. Her voice shaking with the depth of her anger, she shouted, "Maybe you should! Maybe this marriage is too premature. Maybe we're not suited at all. Right now I'm no longer sure I even want to marry someone as controlling as you!"

The silence that followed her outburst was thunderous. When James finally spoke his tone was deadly calm and rang with coldness. "Maybe you're not the only one unsure of this marriage, and maybe you are right. You shouldn't marry me. Good night, Lauren."

Once in This Lifetime
(Five Brothers: Book 2)

<u>Excerpt</u>

"Excuse me, miss. Did you happen to notice a young woman sitting at the table ahead of you a few moments ago?"

The voice was gentle, quiet, like the words issued forth effortlessly yet with a depth of sound that was thunder and caress at the same time. Julia shivered, the sound of that voice sliding down her spine like silk over skin. Tilting her head back, way back, she looked a long way up and her gaze got kidnapped by the bluest, most brilliant eyes she'd ever beheld. He wasn't a brother after all—at least not a black brother. That realization was quickly followed by awareness that he was an attractive man. Well, without the blue eyes he was attractive; with them he was arresting. He was blond, with hair low cut like a military man. His thick eyebrows were straight, nearly meeting above the bridge of his long, narrow nose, the rounded tip relieving it of beak-like prominence. His eyelashes, thick and long from what Julia could tell with him looking downwards and them fluttering as he blinked slightly, would be a sight to behold with him in repose and them reclining just above his cheekbones. His lips, firm and thin would have been overlooked what with his blue eyes taking center stage. But they were quirked in the cutest way, kicking up at the left corner slightly as if amusement was tipping them helplessly upward. That last thought moved her from her mesmerized state and made her realize that she'd been captivated by a man, something that she never did—at least not since that marriage—and by a white man too. *That* certainly had never happened before. She'd always preferred a hint of brown.

Someone Like You
(Five Brothers: Book 3)
<u>Excerpt</u>

"I never asked you out!" She sounded appalled. Either she really was or was a pretender. He went with the latter since she was female.

"You implied that you wanted *me* to ask *you* out. Wasn't that the purpose of all that talk about my intentions towards you—that is, getting me to take you on a date?"

"You're delusional." Even as she said it, Stacy wasn't sure she believed it. Was that what she had subconsciously been trying to do? Despite his cynicism, downright down-on-women attitude, and outright rudeness sometimes, Nate Roach was interesting, and she did want to go out with him. There was just one thing to fix first. "You didn't do it right."

"Do what right?" His voice was wary like he thought she'd lost all cranial control.

"Ask me out properly," she told him.

"I don't know what's proper. I don't do this—dating, I mean. Truthfully, I don't want to do this. I just want my Bible back, and this seems like the best way to get it." Nate knew it wasn't true as soon as he said it. She fascinated him although he was fighting it. With her verve, she was an engaging conversationalist, a captivating phone companion. He had fun talking to her, sparring with her, and fielding her verbal volleys. He felt alive, like he hadn't felt in years in female company. He wanted to see her. He just didn't want her to know what he really wanted.

"Okay," she was saying now, "I'll help you. Repeat after me,

'Stacy, will you go on a date with me tomorrow night?'"

"I will not," he growled uncooperatively.

Stacy sighed. "Obviously you're not a romantic. A gi—

"*Obviously*," he interrupted in a *perish-the-thought* tone.

"A girl just likes to hear the words. It's nicer that way," she explained, her tone suggesting he was slow.

"I just want my Bible back."

"So you don't want to go on the date."

"That's a means to an end."

"Right. To get the Bible back." A coil of annoyance started in Stacy's abdomen. He could at least pretend to be interested. Suddenly, she didn't want to see him. She was interested, but not desperate. If he wasn't interested, why should she put herself and him through a date that would be a trial for both of them? "You know what, Nate, come to Queens to get the Bible. I don't want to go out with you. Is this your cell?"

"Yes," he said slowly, like he was unsure whether he was coming or going.

"Good. I'll text my address to you. Good night."

Nate looked angrily at his iPhone's screen. Why did women have to be so contrary, complicated, and downright difficult? He swore they did it on purpose. He was very offended that after putting words into his mouth to invite her out, she'd refused when he did. She had sounded miffed too. He wondered what had upset *her*. He hadn't said a thing that he could think of. His phone beeped. It was a text message with her address. She lived in Rosedale. She had the nerve to tell him to come at seven o'clock sharp tomorrow evening. Nate decided to watch the news instead of going to bed. He was too irritated.

Not His Choice
(Five Brothers: Book 4)
Excerpt

"The SAB stands for Second Advent Believers," she explained the acronym.

"I know."

"You're familiar with the denomination?"

"I would say so. I'm one of them."

Her eyes widened, and then her tiny lips split into a wide, pleasure-filled smile. "That's wonderful! Which conference are you with? Tri-State?"

The sliver of a smile that had been chasing the fringes of his mouth faded. She should have stopped at 'That's wonderful.' Although no one spoke about it, the SAB church still worshipped for the most part along racial lines—black and whites separately. The membership in Tri-State was predominantly black and in Northern mostly white. The fact that she concluded he was a Tri-State member because he was black said she thought stereotypically and worse still, it rang with racism.

"Wouldn't it be nice to stomp that stereotype out cold and throw that bigoted conclusion back in your face if I were to say I'm a member of your lily-white conference?"

Pamela could only sit and stare in shock at his scorn-laden words and the deep dislike in his eyes. Her thoughts tripped over themselves in reverse, trying to see what she'd said to set him off. Stereotype? Bigoted conclusion? Was he calling her a racist? For sure with the words 'lily-white' conference.

Shaken and at a loss for words, Pam scrambled in her vocabulary and found some to string together in a quivery statement. "I-I'm s-sorry, although I'm not sure what I'm apologizing for. Obviously, I offended you with something I said, and it wasn't my intent to do that."

He pushed his chair back and stood. Leveling a hostile look at her, he bit out, "It's never the intent of your people to offend; it's just inherent in your nature to do it." Giving her a killer look, he stalked away.

Your people? Pam's breath caught at the insult. Now who was being offensive? She stared at his departing back. Temper suddenly kicked her in the stomach, and then booted her in the rear end. She sailed off the seat in hot pursuit of that man, a mouthful of set-downs on the tip of her tongue.

Threading her way through the diners, she caught him just before he entered the kitchen. "Excuse me," she said, detaining him with a hand on his arm.

He stopped, sliced a carving-knife sharp look at her and dropped his gaze pointedly to her hand.

He deserved irritation. He'd made her mad. Why should she be the only one aggravated? Pam kept her hand in place and started talking. "You know nothing about me, so before you cast aspersions on my character, I suggest you find out who I am or keep your insults to yourself. First off, I'm no bigot. I've found that those quick to accuse others of prejudice are themselves prejudiced. Now, if I said something to offend you, be a man and tell me what it is instead of flying into a fit and being an ass."

Rage made your vision change colors. Peter hadn't believed it until this moment. Through a haze of red, battling an overwhelming desire to throttle the woman in front of him, he growled through his teeth. "TAKE. YOUR. HAND. OFF. MY. ARM."

Something in his face must have made her wise up, although she didn't look scared. She removed her hand.

They had an audience now. They hadn't been shouting, but anger had its unique octave and it attracted attention. The diners nearest to them watched with avid interest and open curiosity. Denny and two volunteers were hovering at the kitchen door. His look said *what in the name of all that's good is going on?* Peter ignored him. He had some final words for this woman. Leveling a glacial glare on Pamela Brinkley he hissed, "Let me make something clear to you, I'm a man and not an ass. Lucky for you, my mother raised me a gentleman. If not for that, you'd be flat on the floor, out cold." Raking a scathing look over her from head to toe, he shouldered his way past Denny and the others into the kitchen. He should have listened to the voice of caution and not approached that woman tonight. What a shrew!

Local Gold
(Five Brothers: Book 5)
Excerpt

"You have to let me go," he murmured, smiling at her.

"I can't. My hands are numb." She grinned at him, knowing this was more than friendly playfulness, but unable to resist flirtation.

"Soooo," he drawled, "I guess we'll stay like this?"

"That's not a bad idea."

"You won't get your bath," he pointed out.

"But I'll get...," She trailed off. *You* was what she was going to say, but she didn't want to be so obvious.

"What will you get?" The question came out in a husky rumble.

When their eyes met, his were filled with the heat of awareness, which Bri could only imagine mirrored hers. Her lips felt dry. She moistened them with her tongue. The action captured his attention. Her breath paused when his eyes fell to her mouth, and then respiring through her nose wasn't enough. Her lips parted, and she exhaled in quick puffs of air and inhaled even faster.

"I think you ought to let me go or..." His voice sounded like sandpaper rubbing on concrete.

"Or what?" Bri whispered. *You'll kiss me?* Her answer would be 'Yes, please'. She didn't find out. Gently, Bart reached up and pulled her hands from around his neck. He placed them carefully in her lap. "I'll go get your bath ready," he said, not answering her question at all. With a longing look at her mouth, he walked away to do what he promised.

A Fall for Grace
(Seneca Mountain Romances: Book 1)
Excerpt

"Solomon, this isn't going to work. I can't—."

"Shh," he said, silencing her negatives and pessimism with a finger against her lips. "I love you," he declared and then repeated it, enunciating the words so there would be no incomprehension, "*I love you*. And I'm not going to let you throw what we have and all we can have away. The Bible tells us to ask, seek, and knock and doors will open for us. I am going to keep asking, seeking, and knocking until you open your heart to me. I'm going to be like that widow who the judge got tired of and just gave her what she wanted. You're the judge. Consider me the petitioner. I'm not going to stop telling you that I love you, that I need you, that I refuse to live my life any more without you until you get tired, surrender and give me what we both want and need."

Looking into his eyes, Grace was captivated by the determination in those dark depths. The intensity of his speech and the sincerity of his words were breaking through the invisible walls of resistance that she'd erected. If he kept at it tonight, she wasn't sure she'd last with this battle against the onslaught of his love. Could she really take a chance on him? Should she take a chance on him? Would she have regrets later if she let him go? If she yielded to the pull and poignancy of this moment, and accepted the love he'd declared, received the permanence with him that he was offering, would she have regrets later?

He pulled her into his arms, letting her feel the hardness of him against her tender places, stirring desire in her heart and in places that should stay asleep until wedded bliss. He kissed the corner of her mouth. "Take a chance on me Grace," he coaxed, his voice a seductively husky sound. It was like he'd read her mind. She felt the foundations of her fortress give way and begin crumbling. "You won't regret it," he promised and whatever barriers she'd set up against him buckled under the weight of his persistence. "I love you, Grace." In her heart, she whispered the same. Aloud she promised to take a chance on him for the second time that week.

A Price Too High
(Seneca Mountain Romances: Book 2)
<u>Excerpt</u>

As it turned out, he was speechless when he opened the door and saw her, but then so was she. The sight of him in a ridged undershirt that outlined every muscle on his chest and showcased his powerful biceps tumbled her thoughts into a steamy memory of tangled sheets, urgent kisses, frenzied caresses, and the mind-blowing passion that they had shared on their sole night together.

He was staring at her stomach like it was a UFO and this was his very first time seeing one. If their roles were reversed, maybe she would be shocked too. Karen passed her tongue over her lips and forced herself to speak. "Hi, Douglas. May I come in?"

Shock sped away fast. His eyes jumped from her belly to her face and the fury blazing in his gaze made Karen cringe. "You lying, scheming, wicked user!" Every vitriolic word barreled through his clenched teeth and slammed Karen like assault weapons' firepower, each hit leaving her fighting for breath and struggling to stay on her feet with the unmasked hatred in them. His voice rising, he accused, "You *left* me on our wedding night, skulking away like a thief without having the decency or courage to tell me to my face how you truly felt about my family and why you had really married me. You sent me an inadequate text message after you fled, leaving me reeling and wondering how you could say you love me, how you could make love with me and then use me as a vessel for revenge. You never returned my numerous calls and then you disconnected your phone. Now seven months later you show up at my door and expect *me* to let *you* in?"

Tears, hot and stinging pooled in her eyes, and her throat ached with the effort not to cry out at the scorn and disdain in her husband's face. She hadn't expected a positive reception, but neither had she been prepared for the magnitude of his venom. By force of will alone, she managed to keep her tears at bay, but her voice still wobbled when she spoke. "I-I n-need to talk to you, Doug. P-please let me in."

He looked at her for a long time, the repugnance in his expression unchanged, before he turned and walked back into the apartment, leaving the door open. Karen bit her lip, thinking that the open door meant she could enter. She crossed the threshold with cautious steps.

All Things Work Together
(Seneca Mountain Romances: Book 3)
<u>Excerpt</u>

I want to talk to you about Adam."

Jasmine's spine stiffened. She knew where this wind was blowing. "What about him?" she asked calmly.

He sat back in his office chair and folded his arms across his chest. "He told me that you confiscated his phone last night."

"Did he tell you why?" Jasmine raised her eyebrows, the question flavored a bit with spunk.

"He was on it after curfew, but th—"

"For the third night in a row," she interrupted, emphasizing the magnitude of the misdeed.

"Yes, I know all that, but that's not the part I have a problem with."

"Oh?" There were parts to this now? And why would he have a problem? Hadn't he been concerned about her maintaining order in his household? Now he had a problem when she fulfilled his wishes?

"When Adam got his phone back there were three international calls made from it. Two to Jamaica and one to St. Thomas."

Jasmine sat statue-still in her chair, hearing the accusation he hadn't articulated. She raised a forefinger, "Wait one minute. If there were international calls on his phone, I didn't make them."

"The times of the calls were when you had the phone in your possession," he pointed out.

He still hadn't accused her outright, but he didn't have to. He believed she made those calls. That was clearer than day. Adam King, Jr. was a crafty boy. She hadn't expected this. Jasmine wouldn't underestimate him again, but if he thought he could intimidate her into not enforcing the rules his dad put in place, he'd better think twice. But first things first. One problem at a time. "Look, Pastor King, I just told you I did not make those calls. Obviously you don't believe me. The fact that you've persisted with the issue by pointing out that I had the phone at the times of the calls, implying that no other person could have made the calls, tells me that you'll believe your son's word over mine. I understand that. I'm a stranger still, and he's your child. However, you might want to consider a couple of things: I have my own phone. Why would I use your son's? The day we met, you doubted whether I understood teenagers or whether I could care for them. At the risk of being insubordinate, I'm now wondering how much *you* understand teenagers?"

He leaned forward in his chair, his expression hard. The chill in his eyes said her words had struck a chord. Jasmine wasn't trying to get fired, but she'd learned it's best to start as you mean to go on. Don't take things docilely, especially when you're not at fault. Be firm, frank, and as much as possible be polite, but speak your mind.

"Have you considered that Adam was the one who made those calls?" she asked.

"Why would he do that?" His tone could turn a water droplet to an icicle.

"Because he was angry that I took his phone, he wanted to get back at me. He probably hoped to intimidate me into not doing it again if he got me in trouble with you."

"You don't know my children like I do, Ms. Lewis. Adam isn't the kind of child to be cunning like that," he objected.

"Sometimes I wonder if you know your children at all, Pastor." Okay she was having a problem with the 'be polite' part. Now the words were out, and she could not take them back. Jasmine didn't try to fix it because she couldn't.

"What's that supposed to mean?" His eyebrows went south and his mouth firmed into a displeased line, annoyance shadowing his expression like storm clouds darkening the skies.

"You work all the time. They don't see you. Do you know that Claire wishes you worked fewer hours so you could spend more time with her? Do you know that Adam sleeps restlessly some nights and cries out for you?" She watched surprise and hurt do a fast exchange in his expression before he camouflaged it. "And do you know that he also cries out for his mother?"

"Enough!" The word struck like thunder, cracking the air like lightning.

Jasmine jerked and watched pain and anger perform a visible struggle in his face. He inhaled a significant portion of the oxygen in the air and exhaled slowly. "I might not know everything there is to know about my kids," he started, his voice tight and his words measured. "And maybe I do need to spend time with them," he continued through his teeth. "But you don't know them period. You don't know any of us. You have no idea what we've been through as a family, what we still go through. Do me a favor and clear it with me before you punish my kids and please don't ever mention their mother again. Goodnight, Ms. Lewis." With that he left his chair and opened the door.

Stunned, she sat there for some moments before grasping that this was a dismissal. She rose slowly and approached the door with even more lethargic steps. At the door she paused, not sure what to say, but feeling compelled to make an exit statement. She looked up at him, but he was staring determinedly at some point beyond her, his jaw like granite. Jasmine wet her lips. "I'm sorry. I didn't mean to stir up old hurts. I was just trying to—"

"Good. Night. Ms. Lewis." The words came out with forceful pace, the emotion in them bordering on violence.

Jasmine sailed out the door. She knew when she had overstayed her welcome.

ABOUT THE AUTHOR

A believer in happy endings and forever after type stories, Brigette has been an avid romance reader since her teens. Inspired by her own real life romance with her husband, Clifford, she began writing romance novels after the birth of her first child and hasn't stopped since. Brigette holds a degree in Cultural Studies with a concentration in communication. Brigette writes Christian Romance and Christian Romantic Suspense. She lives in the northeastern U.S.A. with her husband and four children. She can be reached at hearthavenbooks@gmail.com or visit her website, www.brigettemanie.com. You can also find her at the links below:

www.amazon.com/Brigette-Manie/e/B00A3CPJC4

https://www.goodreads.com/author/show/6562932.Brigette_Manie

https://www.facebook.com/brigette.manie.author?ref=stream

https://twitter.com/BrigetteManie

CPSIA information can be obtained at www.ICGtesting.com
Printed in the USA
LVOW06s2138260715

447744LV00008B/117/P